VIRGINIA STONE

The Correspondent — A Tale of Silent Letters

First edition

This book was professionally typeset on Reedsy.
Find out more at reedsy.com

Contents

1

Prologue

The rain fell relentlessly against the windows of the cottage, tapping softly like a thousand tiny fingers urging Alex to listen. The small house, nestled on the edge of Harrowsfield, felt both alien and strangely comforting. She had come here seeking silence, seeking escape, but the stillness left her alone with the ghosts of her past.

Alex stared out the window, watching the heavy clouds blanket the sky. It was hard to believe that only a few weeks ago, she had been in the city, caught in the rhythm of a life she no longer recognized as her own. But that life felt so far away now. She'd left it all behind: the career, the chaos, the memories.

She thought of her apartment, packed with echoes of a life that no longer fit. Thought of the people who had once surrounded her — friends, colleagues, even lovers — but none of them had known her. Not really. Not the way she needed to be known.

The past was a strange thing. One moment, it felt like it was pushing her forward, the next, it was holding her back, clawing at her like an open wound. And no matter how hard she tried, no matter how far she ran, it was always there.

Was I running away, or just running in circles?

She wasn't sure.

Alex took a deep breath, trying to clear the weight from her chest. The silence in the house was suffocating at times. It had been a year since everything changed. A year since the accident that had shattered her world. Her fingers instinctively reached for the stack of blank paper on the table beside her. Writing had always been her way of coping, of understanding the things that couldn't be understood.

She pulled a sheet of paper from the stack, the crisp edges familiar beneath her fingertips. As the pen touched the paper, the weight in her chest loosened just a little. But the words that came were not the ones she expected.

Dear Jordan...

The name felt like a stone in her throat. She hadn't thought about Jordan in years. Not since that final, bitter argument that had torn their friendship apart. They had been inseparable once, two sides of the same coin, their bond stronger than any of the other relationships she had ever had. But that was before the truth came out, before the lies, the misunderstandings, the things they had both failed to say.

Her mind wandered back to those days. She could still remember the late nights, their laughter spilling into the early morning hours, the way

Jordan's smile had always made her feel like the world was still good. How could she have ever thought it would end like that? How could she have let it?

I don't know why I'm writing to you. I can't even remember the last time we spoke, but I remember everything about you. About us. I remember the way you used to make me laugh when everything else felt too heavy. But I'm not sure you would even remember me now. After everything that happened...

The pen trembled in her hand as memories flooded in. Alex hadn't been able to face the loss of their friendship — the way it had ended without warning, like a door slamming shut. She had been angry, but more than that, she had been hurt. She hadn't known how to fix it, and in the end, she hadn't tried.

I think I've spent more time thinking about what happened than anything else in my life. And maybe that's the problem. I spent so long wondering how it went wrong that I lost sight of what was right between us. I never told you that I was sorry, and I should have. I should have said it long before now.

As the pen moved across the page, a wave of exhaustion washed over her. Not the physical kind, but the kind that settled deep in her bones. The weight of years spent running from herself. From the truth.

She paused, looking out the window again. The quiet town was starting to settle into the evening — the last traces of sunlight fading behind the horizon. And yet, the longer she stayed here, the more it felt like the past was alive, lurking in the corners, waiting for her to confront it.

Her thoughts drifted to another time. A time before Harrowsfield. Before the house, the isolation, the letters.

Flashback

It was a Monday morning when the call came. The kind of call that shakes your foundation, that rips apart everything you thought you knew. Alex had been in the office, sorting through emails, the hum of fluorescent lights overhead, when her phone buzzed. The name on the screen — a number she hadn't recognized.

She picked it up, thinking it was another sales pitch, or perhaps a wrong number. But the voice on the other end was familiar.

"Alex, I need you to come to the hospital. Now."

It was her brother, Sam. His voice sounded strained, clipped, like he was holding something back.

"The car... it's... mom and dad. They're gone, Alex. It's... it's an accident."

She had been in shock for days. The funeral, the phone calls, the sympathy. The pitying looks from strangers who thought they understood. They didn't. No one did. Not until you felt the cold, finality of it yourself. The emptiness that followed, like a shadow that would never leave.

It wasn't just that her parents were gone. It was everything else that had been left unsaid, the decades of distance, of things left to fester. She had never told them how much they meant to her. She had never apologized for the years of stubbornness, the way she had shut them out. And now, it was too late.

Alex blinked, pushing the memory away as quickly as it came.

The letter she had started now felt too personal, too raw. Her mind was a tangled mess of what had been and what could never be again. But it was also a reminder of something she'd known for a long time. Her past wasn't finished with her. It wasn't ever going to be.

A sudden noise broke her from her thoughts — the sound of something shifting in the next room. Alex froze, her pen still hovering above the paper. It was probably the wind, or an old floorboard settling, but something about the moment made her feel as if the house itself was holding its breath.

She stood up, the sudden rush of unease crawling up her spine. Her gaze moved across the room, but everything appeared still. Normal. She swallowed hard, trying to shake off the feeling. But as she moved toward the door, she glanced down at the letter once more.

And that's when she saw it.

A letter. Not hers. But there it was, resting on the table in front of her.

It was the same handwriting. Jordan's handwriting.

2

Chapter 1: The Escape

Alex had always thought she could outrun her past. But now, as she stood before the old wooden house in Harrowsfield, a small town tucked far from the reaches of the city, she wondered if perhaps she had been running in circles. The air here felt different—fresh and clean, filled with the scent of pine trees and damp earth. It was a far cry from the choking smog and constant noise of the city she had left behind, a city where she'd spent too many years distracting herself from what was broken inside her.

The house was smaller than she had imagined, tucked away on the outskirts of town with ivy climbing the weathered walls. It looked like it belonged in a painting, a peaceful scene of quiet retreat. There was no way anyone could find her here. No one knew her name, no one knew her story. It was exactly what she needed.

The door creaked as she pushed it open, her eyes scanning the modest interior. A small living room with faded wallpaper, an old couch, and a fireplace that seemed to have lost its warmth years ago. The kitchen was just as simple, functional yet devoid of any charm or comfort. But that was all right. Alex didn't need comfort. What she needed was silence.

The kind of silence that would let her breathe again.

She set her suitcase down, the weight of it a reminder of everything she had left behind. It wasn't just the city. It wasn't just the career she'd spent years building, only to see it crumble. It wasn't even the loss of relationships that never truly healed. No, it was the memories. The accident. The phone call that had shattered everything.

It had been just another Tuesday when she received the call. Alex had been on her way to an interview when her phone buzzed with an unknown number. At first, she thought it was spam—another telemarketer, another pointless interruption. But then the voice on the other end stopped her in her tracks.

"Alex, I need you to come to the hospital. Now."

Her brother Sam. His voice was ragged, like he had been crying, but there was no time to question it. The urgency in his tone was enough.

When she arrived at the hospital, the world felt like it was crumbling around her. Her parents had been in a car accident. They were gone. Just like that.

She hadn't been close to them in years, but that didn't mean the loss didn't carve through her. The funeral had been a blur—people offering condolences she didn't want, the hollow stares from family members who barely knew who she was anymore. It was too much to take in at once, too overwhelming. And in the aftermath, Alex had buried herself in her work, hoping that the chaos of her career would drown out the emptiness gnawing at her insides.

Back in Harrowsfield, Alex shook the memory away. She didn't want to think about it anymore. She had come here for a fresh start, and the past was no longer a part of the plan.

Her eyes drifted to the small table by the window. The stack of blank paper she had brought with her sat there, waiting. For what? She wasn't sure yet. The idea of writing had come to her in the weeks leading up to the move. A way to make sense of everything. To put it all down on paper and try to understand the chaos that had become her life.

She pulled a chair out from under the table and sat down, the wood groaning under the weight of her body. Reaching for the pen, she hesitated. Where to start? She had so many people she had lost touch with. So many people who had once meant everything to her. So many things left unsaid.

The first name that came to mind was Jordan.

Jordan.

Her heart tightened at the thought. It had been years since they had last spoken. Their friendship had been everything once. But somewhere along the way, somewhere between the heartbreak and the hurt, it had all gone wrong. The argument. The silence. Neither one of them had ever bothered to fix it, and now it was too late. Or so it seemed.

With a deep breath, Alex set the pen to paper.

Dear Jordan,

I don't know why I'm writing to you. After everything that happened between us, I think we both know it's too late for apologies. I think we both know that we've moved on, or at least, I thought I had. But the truth is, I've spent more time wondering what went wrong than anything else. Maybe writing to you will help me let go of that. Maybe it won't.

I remember the late nights we used to spend talking about everything and nothing, the way you always knew how to make me laugh when I was sure I was losing my mind. It feels like another lifetime now, but I think I've always missed that, more than anything. I miss you. I miss the person I was when I was with you.

Alex stopped and looked at the letter, her throat tight. This wasn't easy. It never would be. But somehow, it felt necessary. And if nothing else, maybe it would give her a chance to feel something other than this constant ache in her chest.

She set the pen down for a moment and rubbed her eyes. The light outside was beginning to fade, casting long shadows across the room.

Her thoughts wandered again. To her parents. To the things she had never told them. To the time lost, never to return.

I wish I had told you more. I wish I hadn't let things fall apart the way they did. I wish I could change it, but I can't.

She remembered their last conversation like it had happened only yesterday. She had been in a rush, as always, juggling too many deadlines and too many expectations. Jordan had called her that day, the same way she always did when they hadn't talked in a while. But this time, it was different. There was something in her voice, something that made Alex pause.

"Are you okay, Alex?" Jordan had asked. "I've been trying to reach you, but you've been avoiding me."

Avoiding her. Alex had tried to brush it off, tried to act as though everything was fine. But it wasn't. It hadn't been for a long time.

They fought. The words were harsh, sharp, and unforgiving. It wasn't just one fight—it was years of unspoken resentment, bottled up until it exploded. And when it was over, neither one of them knew how to fix it.

That was the last time they spoke. The silence that followed had been deafening.

Alex shook her head as she set the pen down again. The past was never far behind her, never completely out of reach. It clung to her, like the shadows in the corners of the room.

She had come here to escape, but perhaps, just perhaps, she couldn't outrun the things she had left undone. Not yet. Not until she faced them. But for now, writing was all she had.

As she placed the letter in the drawer, a sense of unease settled in her chest. It was too quiet. Too still.

But then, a strange sound broke the silence. The soft rustle of paper. Alex froze. She turned toward the desk, her heart beginning to race.

There, sitting on the table where the letter had just been, was another letter. It wasn't hers.

Her name was written on the front. In the same handwriting. Jordan's handwriting.

3

Chapter 2: The First Letter

Alex sat at the small, wooden table in the cottage, the warm glow of the afternoon sun filtering through the window. The quiet of Harrowsfield felt like a blanket—soft, heavy, and all-encompassing. Outside, the gentle sway of the trees in the wind seemed to hum in rhythm with the silence inside the house. But despite the peace, there was still something inside her that felt unsettled. Something unspoken, unfinished.

She had been here for a few days now, unpacking the remnants of her life into this new place. The act of physically moving was easy, a distraction. But the mind? It was relentless. There were too many things left behind. Too many people. And one person, in particular, whose absence haunted her more than the others.

Jordan.

The name hung in the air like a shadow. It had been years since they last spoke, but it felt like only yesterday that their friendship had been shattered. A cruel argument, a moment of silence, and then—nothing.

Alex thought of all the things she wished she could have said to Jordan before everything fell apart. The apology she had never given, the truth she had never voiced. She could have tried to fix it. But in the end, she had walked away, just as Jordan had. And for so long, she had told herself it was easier this way—easier to forget, easier to move on.

But now, here, in this house where no one knew her, the past had a way of creeping back into her thoughts. She couldn't outrun it, no matter how far she ran. And so, she sat in front of a blank sheet of paper, staring at it with a sense of dread.

A part of her wondered why she was even bothering to write. What was the point of sending a letter to someone she would never speak to again? But it felt necessary. Therapeutic, even. Maybe this was the only way to put it all to rest. To release what had been sitting like a stone in her chest for all these years.

With a shaky breath, Alex picked up the pen. Her fingers hovered over the paper for a moment. She wasn't sure where to start. How to begin to tell someone everything she had never said.

Dear Jordan,

I don't even know where to begin. It feels strange, writing to you like this after all this time. After everything that happened between us. It feels like there's too much to say, too much left undone. But here I am, writing it down, even though I know you'll never read it.

I remember the way we used to talk for hours, about everything and nothing. You were always the one who could make me laugh, even when everything felt like it was falling apart. We used to joke that nothing could break us apart. But, somehow, it did.

I don't know what happened, Jordan. I don't know why it turned out the way it did. I've spent so much time wondering, trying to figure it out. But the truth is, I don't think I ever really understood you, or maybe you never understood me. I don't know. All I know is, I miss you. I miss the friendship we had. And I regret how it ended.

I never told you how much you meant to me. How much I depended on you. How much I loved you. Not in the way you think, but in a way that was deeper, truer than anything I've ever known. But I never said it. And now I never will. And I don't know how to live with that.

Alex stopped writing, the weight of the words too heavy to continue. Her heart pounded in her chest, a mix of regret and relief. It was strange, how cathartic writing could be. The act of putting everything down, even if it was just for herself, felt like releasing a burden she had carried for far too long. But it didn't fix anything. It didn't change what had been broken.

She sighed and placed the pen down on the table, staring at the letter for a moment before folding it neatly. It wasn't perfect, but it was a start. Maybe that was all she could hope for—a small beginning.

Just then, her phone buzzed on the table. Startled, Alex reached for it, wondering who could be calling or messaging her. She didn't know anyone here. She had deliberately kept her distance from her old life, hoping the silence would be enough to drown out the noise.

The phone screen showed an unknown number. Her finger hovered over the screen, hesitating. Who could it be? A wrong number? A solicitor? She almost let it ring out, but something made her pick it up.

"Hello?" she said, her voice tentative.

There was a long pause on the other end before a voice broke through, slow and deliberate, almost like it was waiting for her to respond.

"Did you ever wonder if writing could change the past?"

Alex froze, the words hanging in the air like a sudden chill. She didn't recognize the voice. It wasn't anyone she knew. The question felt... out of place. The hairs on the back of her neck prickled, and for a brief moment, she felt like she was standing on the edge of something she couldn't quite see.

"Who is this?" she asked, but the line went dead before she could hear an answer. The phone screen went dark, the call ended without explanation.

Alex sat there, staring at the screen. The words echoed in her mind.

Did you ever wonder if writing could change the past?

A shiver ran down her spine. It was a strange, cryptic message—one that made no sense, yet felt oddly familiar. Almost as if it was meant for her.

But she couldn't dwell on it now. The letter to Jordan had been enough to unravel something inside her. The past was starting to seep back into her thoughts, like a river breaking through a dam. And she wasn't sure if she was ready to face it.

As the silence of the house settled around her again, Alex couldn't help but wonder if that voice on the phone was just a coincidence. Or if it was something more. A sign, maybe. A reminder that no matter how far she tried to run, her past wasn't done with her.

4

Chapter 3: A Strange Response

The morning light crept through the curtains, casting soft patterns on the wooden floors. Alex woke with a sense of quiet relief, the remnants of a dream fading just beyond her reach. For a moment, the world felt calm again, as though the strange feeling that had settled over her the night before had been just a fleeting thought. A question, a voice on the other end of the phone, and then silence.

The events of the previous day felt distant now, almost unreal. The letter to Jordan sat on the table, still unopened. Alex had left it there, unsure whether it was worth sending or even revisiting. But the act of writing had given her something—if not closure, then at least a chance to breathe. And that was all she could ask for, wasn't it?

She stretched, her body aching in places she hadn't noticed before, a reminder of the months of tension and stress she had carried with her. But now, she was free. At least, that's what she told herself as she shuffled into the kitchen, the quiet hum of the house surrounding her.

Alex made her way to the small counter, where a kettle sat, waiting to be filled. She reached for a cup, trying to shake off the remnants of the unsettling conversation from the night before. She was alone here, far from the noise of her old life. The world outside felt untouched by her pain. This was her time. Her space.

As she prepared her coffee, she glanced at the table.

The letter. The one to Jordan.

Except now, there was another letter. A new one.

It sat innocently on the kitchen table, placed directly in front of the chair where she had written her own letter the night before. Alex's heart skipped a beat as she stared at it. The envelope was simple—no address, no stamp. Just her name, written neatly in black ink, across the front.

Her name.

But it wasn't just the fact that there was a letter. It was the handwriting. It looked almost identical to hers.

Alex froze, her breath caught in her throat. Her eyes scanned the paper, the edges sharp and precise, the letters perfectly formed, as though someone had copied her own handwriting.

She didn't know why, but a cold shiver crawled up her spine as she approached the table. She could feel her pulse quickening, the air thick with the strange sensation that had clung to her the night before.

This isn't possible, she thought. *I must be imagining things.*

But even as she thought it, the truth was already in front of her. The letter was real. And it was there. For no reason she could understand.

With a hesitant hand, she picked it up, the weight of it feeling too solid for a figment of her imagination. Slowly, she tore open the envelope and unfolded the paper inside.

Her eyes scanned the words.

Dear Alex,

It's strange, writing to you after all this time. I never thought we would end up here, separated by nothing more than silence and misunderstandings. I'm sure you've spent countless nights wondering where things went wrong, just as I have. I'm sorry, more than you'll ever know, for the things I never said. But even though it's too late now, I hope that maybe, just maybe, you'll find it in yourself to forgive me.

I've missed you more than you can imagine. And I regret everything we never had the chance to fix.

The words hung in the air like a slow, deliberate heartbeat. Alex's hand trembled slightly as she held the paper in her fingers. It felt too real. Too... familiar.

She read the letter again, her mind struggling to comprehend what she was seeing. *Did I write this?* she wondered. But no—she hadn't. She had written her own letter, a letter that had remained on the table, untouched. This one, the one in front of her, was not hers. It couldn't be.

But the handwriting. It was identical. The words, the tone—it was as if someone had written the very things she had wanted to say, the things she had never been able to.

Her thoughts raced. *Could it be a coincidence?*

But she knew, deep down, that it wasn't. There was no way this was a mistake.

Alex stood there for a long moment, the letter still clutched in her hand. The calm she had felt when she first woke up was gone now, replaced by a creeping sense of confusion. What was happening? How could this letter have appeared? Why had it been placed exactly where she had written her own?

The more she thought about it, the more it didn't make sense. *It's just a coincidence,* she told herself again. *I must have written it and forgotten.*

But deep down, she didn't believe it. The way the handwriting matched her own was uncanny. It was too precise, too deliberate. And the words—the apology, the regret—they mirrored exactly what she had written, yet something about this felt off. Like she was looking at a reflection of herself she didn't recognize.

Alex sat down, her mind swirling with the possibilities. Could it be real? Could Jordan have somehow written this letter? Had she come to find her, after all these years?

But no. That didn't make sense. Jordan hadn't contacted her in years. There was no way she could have known what Alex had written, what had been said, or even where Alex was now. And yet, the letter felt too personal, too real to dismiss.

She set the letter down, her hands trembling. As she reached for the cup of coffee she had forgotten about, her phone buzzed on the table. The sudden sound startled her, and for a brief moment, she wondered if her heart had skipped a beat.

It was an unknown number again.

Not again, she thought. *I can't deal with this right now.*

Her fingers hovered over the phone, but something made her pick it up. She pressed the green button, bringing it to her ear.

The voice on the other end was distorted, as if it were underwater, the words slow, deliberate.

"Did you ever wonder if writing could change the past?"

Alex's breath caught in her throat. She didn't recognize the voice. It wasn't anyone she knew. The question came again, this time even more unsettling than before.

Without thinking, she ended the call. Her mind was racing now, her pulse quickening with every unanswered question. The letter. The phone call. The voice. All of it. It couldn't be a coincidence anymore.

And yet, part of her wanted to believe it was.

The room felt suddenly colder, the silence pressing down on her. She looked at the letter again, its words echoing in her mind.

And in the pit of her stomach, a deep sense of dread began to settle.

5

Chapter 4: Letters to the Past

The morning after the strange voicemail and the inexplicable letter, Alex sat in front of the table again. The house felt eerily quiet, as though it had taken on a life of its own in the wake of the strange events. She had tried to dismiss it all—the letter, the cryptic message, the unnerving feeling that had settled deep in her bones—but the unease wouldn't let her go. It lingered in the air like a low hum, just beneath the surface of the silence.

She pushed the letter from Jordan aside. She couldn't make sense of it, and right now, she needed to focus on something that felt at least somewhat under her control. She needed to write.

After all, that was why she had come here, wasn't it? To heal. To confront the past that she had buried beneath the weight of years. Writing had always been her escape, the way she sorted through the chaos of her mind.

So, she wrote.

This time, she didn't hesitate. The pen moved across the paper with a sense of urgency, as if the words had been waiting to escape for too long. She began with her family—her mother, her father, Sam, her brother. There was so much left unsaid between them. So many things left unspoken.

> *Dear Mom,*
>
> *I never told you how much you meant to me. How much I depended on you, even when I was too stubborn to admit it. I regret the time I wasted being angry, being resentful. You were always there for me, and I was too blind to see it. Maybe I'll never be able to tell you that now, but writing this helps, in some small way.*

I'm sorry. For everything I never said. For every moment I took for granted.

The words were raw, but there was something freeing about them. Even though her mother was gone, even though the chance to say these things was lost, the act of writing them down made Alex feel a little less weighted. A little less alone.

She set the letter aside and started on the next one. This time, it was to her father.

Dear Dad,

I'm sorry we never had the relationship I always wanted. You were always so distant, so wrapped up in your own world. I know we never connected the way I imagined we could have. But you were my father, and I needed you in ways I never knew how to express.

I'm sorry for resenting you, for not understanding. Maybe you weren't perfect, but neither was I.

I hope you found peace before you left. I hope I can, too.

Each letter felt like a piece of the past being laid bare, exposed for the first time. It wasn't about fixing things anymore; it was about acknowledging them. Acknowledging the gaps, the misunderstandings, the regrets.

Alex could feel the weight of the years lifting, bit by bit, with each letter she wrote. But even as the catharsis washed over her, a new kind of tension began to build. Something was changing.

She had noticed it first yesterday. A picture, one of her parents from their younger days, hanging crooked on the wall near the kitchen. At first, she thought it was just her mind playing tricks on her, but as she looked closer, she saw it—the frame was tilted in a way that it hadn't been the day before.

It was small, insignificant, really. But in the silence of the house, it was enough to make her heart skip a beat.

Today, it was the old stack of letters that sat on the bookshelf. Letters that she had brought with her from her old apartment, letters from past friends and acquaintances, some unopened, others marked with the passage of time. As Alex looked at the shelf, she noticed that one of the letters—one she was sure had been buried beneath the others—was now sitting on top, its envelope worn with age, the handwriting on it unmistakable.

Her pulse quickened.

The letter was from Tom. Her old friend from college. She hadn't thought about him in years. He had moved across the country after their friendship ended abruptly, another casualty of her inability to keep the relationships that once mattered to her. She never had the courage to reach out after he left. It felt like everything was always too late, too far gone.

Why is this here? Alex wondered. *I didn't even bring this with me.*

With shaking hands, she pulled it from the shelf, her breath catching in her throat. She had to know what it said. But when she opened it, the message was nothing like what she expected.

The letter inside was dated from years ago, the same year Tom left. Alex read it, her eyes scanning the familiar, slanted handwriting.

> *Dear Alex,*
>
> *I'm sorry I left without saying goodbye. I know it was sudden, and I know it hurt you. I didn't mean for it to, but I had to go. I hope you understand. And I hope you know that even though we lost touch, I've never forgotten you. I think of you often, and I regret how things ended. I hope one day, maybe, we can talk again. But until then, I'll always be grateful for the time we had.*

Alex stared at the letter, the words blurring before her eyes. She hadn't even realized she was holding her breath until her lungs screamed for air. How had this letter gotten here? Why now?

She closed her eyes for a moment, trying to steady herself. It didn't make sense. Tom had been gone for years. He'd never come back. But somehow, this letter had appeared out of nowhere. Just like the letter from Jordan. Just like the phone call from the night before.

The small changes were adding up, like pieces of a puzzle she didn't understand. First the picture, now the letter. What was happening to her?

She tried to push the unsettling thoughts aside and picked up her pen again. But before she could continue, she heard a faint noise—a soft scratching sound, almost like paper being moved.

Her head snapped up, eyes darting across the room. The sound stopped as suddenly as it had started.

The room was still. Quiet.

But the sense of something shifting, something out of place, remained. Alex's pulse began to race again. Something was happening. Something she couldn't explain.

The letter was in her hand, but her mind was somewhere else, piecing together the fragments that didn't quite fit. The house had been quiet when she first arrived, peaceful in its isolation. But now? Now it felt as though something was watching her, waiting for her to uncover what she didn't understand.

With a deep breath, she folded the letter from Tom and returned it to the shelf, not sure what to make of it. The day had started with hope, with the quiet promise of healing. But now, as the sun began to set and the shadows stretched longer across the room, Alex wasn't sure if she was escaping anything at all—or if she was simply walking deeper into a mystery she wasn't ready to face.

6

Chapter 5: The First Shift

The next morning, the house felt different. Alex had woken earlier than usual, the thin light of dawn creeping through the blinds. It wasn't the stillness that was unsettling — no, the stillness had become something Alex could almost welcome, something that felt familiar. It was something else. A quiet tension hung in the air, an intangible weight that settled around her shoulders like a cloak. She couldn't shake it.

The events of the past few days — the letters, the strange changes, the phone calls — lingered in her mind like puzzle pieces she couldn't quite fit together. And there was the voicemail. That voice, asking her if writing could change the past. It felt like an impossible question, yet it had stayed with her, nagging at her in the silence of the house. Could writing really change the past? Could it really reshape memories, reshape reality itself?

She shook the thought away and walked to the kitchen, the routine of making coffee grounding her for a moment. The hot steam from the kettle filled the room, but the nagging sensation of something being off wouldn't leave her. It was like walking through a dream where you knew you were missing something, but you couldn't remember what it was.

Alex stood at the counter, staring at the old coffee pot for a long moment. It was a piece of her mother's old kitchenware, something she had kept after the funeral. She had held onto so many things, as if the objects themselves might bring her closer to the woman who had raised her — the woman she had never truly understood. The woman who had always been just a little too distant, too private, too wrapped up in her own struggles for Alex to see.

It wasn't until her mother's death that Alex realized how much she had longed for that connection. But it was too late. And now, the weight of unspoken words and regret pressed down on her more than ever.

She hadn't written a letter to her mother yet. She had written letters to so many people—friends, ex-lovers, family—but her mother had been the one person she hadn't been able to bring herself to write to. The one letter that felt impossible.

But today, as the house felt colder than usual, Alex knew it was time.

She walked back to the table, her fingers brushing over the pen and the blank page in front of her. For a moment, she hesitated, the inkling of doubt rising in her mind. Could she really do this? Could she really put down everything she had never said? Could she write the words she had been holding onto for so long?

But something inside her pushed the hesitation aside. She had to try. Maybe this would help. Maybe it wouldn't change anything, but it would be something. A way to confront the ghosts of her past.

She picked up the pen.

> *Dear Mom,*
>
> *I've been avoiding this letter for so long. I don't even know where to begin. You've always been a mystery to me, in a way. Not in the sense that I didn't know you — I did. But there were parts of you I never understood, parts of you I never even tried to see. I was*

> *angry with you, and I didn't even know why. I was angry that you never opened up to me the way I wanted, that you never showed me your vulnerabilities the way I thought you should have.*
>
> *But now, I see it. Now I realize that your silence wasn't weakness. It was strength. You carried things alone because you had to. You were always the one who took care of everything — me, Dad, the house. I never realized how much you did until it was too late.*
>
> *I'm sorry. I'm sorry for not understanding, for not being there when you needed me to be.*
>
> *I've been angry for so long, but I don't want to carry that anger anymore. I just want to be able to let it go. Maybe I can't ever fix what was left unsaid, but I can try. I want you to know that I love you. I think I always have, even when I didn't know how to show it.*

Alex put the pen down, the weight of the letter sinking in. It was raw, more than anything she had written before. But it wasn't enough. It didn't feel like closure. She knew that, deep down, nothing would ever feel like closure.

With a sigh, she folded the letter and placed it in the drawer with the others. She didn't know if she would ever send any of them. But for now, writing them was enough. It was all she had.

As she moved around the house, tidying up the kitchen and trying to distract herself from the overwhelming emotions that threatened to flood her, she noticed something.

The photo.

It was a picture of her mother and father, taken long before Alex was born. Her mother's arm draped around her father's shoulders, their faces young and full of promise. Alex had always kept that photo on the windowsill above the sink, a piece of the past she didn't dare to move.

But now? It was gone.

Her heart skipped a beat. She could have sworn she had seen it there just yesterday, but now, it wasn't. She checked the counter, the table, the shelves. Nothing.

It wasn't like her to misplace things. She was careful, always meticulous about where she put things. And yet, the photo was nowhere to be found.

Did I move it? she thought, trying to remember. *Maybe I moved it last night without thinking.*

But as she scanned the room once more, something caught her eye. In the far corner, just beside the small bookshelf that held the letters she had been writing, the photo was sitting—slightly askew, as though it had been placed there recently.

She took a cautious step toward it, her fingers lightly grazing the edges of the frame. It felt colder than it should, as if it had been moved without her noticing.

Her breath caught in her throat. The photo was supposed to be on the windowsill. There was no reason for it to be here.

She stared at it for a moment longer, her mind racing with possibilities. It was silly, really. People moved things around all the time without thinking. But for some reason, this felt wrong. Too strange to ignore.

The hair on the back of her neck prickled. She was about to leave the room when she spotted something else—an old, silver spoon resting on the countertop. It wasn't just any spoon. It was a family heirloom. One that had belonged to her mother. She knew it well; it had always been in the kitchen, part of a set her mother had kept for special occasions. But now, it was sitting in a place it shouldn't be, resting beside the sink as if someone had left it there recently.

Alex's stomach churned. *What is happening?*

Her pulse quickened as she turned toward the window, trying to shake off the unsettling feeling that had taken root in her chest. The quiet of the house seemed to press in on her, the air thick with something she couldn't explain. Had she been imagining things? Was her mind playing tricks on her, worn thin from the isolation?

The changes were small, but they were enough. Enough to make her question everything.

Could it be possible? Could she really be rewriting her own reality with these letters? Or was it something else? Something she couldn't understand?

As she looked around the room once more, trying to steady her breathing, she realized she was no longer sure of what was real. What was shifting. Or if it was all in her head.

7

Chapter 6: The Correspondent

It was early afternoon when Alex found the letter. The day was cold, a sharp wind blowing in from the hills outside, rattling the old windows of the cottage. She had spent the morning organizing the letters she had written—sorting them into neat piles, trying to make sense of the emotions that had been spilling out of her for the past week. Each one was a piece of her past, each one a way to say the things she could never say aloud.

She had finished writing to her late mother that morning, leaving the letter tucked safely in the drawer with the others. There was a strange sense of closure in that act, even though she knew it wasn't enough. It never would be. She had thought about writing more letters, to other family members, maybe even to friends she had left behind, but something held her back. There were just too many things that couldn't be fixed with words.

It was when she was about to go upstairs for a break that she noticed the letter on the table. It wasn't there when she had started her work earlier. She had been in the kitchen, making tea, and the letter was nowhere to be seen. But now, there it was, sitting in front of her, placed neatly on top of the pile of papers she had been working on.

Her heart skipped a beat.

It was an envelope, unmarked. No stamp, no address. Just her name, written in black ink. The handwriting was so familiar, it made her stomach drop. It looked almost identical to her own.

Alex reached for the letter, her fingers trembling. Her mind raced with possibilities. Had she written this letter in some fog of exhaustion, forgotten about it, and left it there? But no. She hadn't written it. She would have remembered. She knew she would.

With shaking hands, she tore open the envelope and unfolded the letter inside.

Dear Alex,

The past is a story you've yet to finish. Will you write it?

That was all.

Alex blinked, staring at the simple, cryptic message. It wasn't signed. There was no explanation. Just that single sentence. The weight of the words settled in her chest, like a stone sinking to the bottom of a deep lake.

The past is a story you've yet to finish.

What did that even mean? Who had sent this? She had no way of knowing. It was written in the same handwriting as the letters she had been writing. But that couldn't be possible. She hadn't told anyone about the letters. She hadn't even planned on mailing any of them. She hadn't shared her thoughts, her struggles, with a soul. So how could someone—anyone—know what she had written?

Her heart pounded in her chest as her mind raced, trying to make sense of the impossible. The idea of someone reading her letters, of someone knowing her deepest thoughts, terrified her. It was as though her most private emotions had been exposed, laid bare for the world to see.

For the next few minutes, Alex sat there, staring at the letter in her hands. She didn't know how long she had been frozen, lost in the confusion that clouded her mind. But slowly, she stood up, her fingers still gripping the letter tightly.

She checked the room again, half-expecting to find someone there. But there was nothing. Just the silence of the house, the stillness of the air.

No one had entered the cottage. No one had come near her. And yet, somehow, someone had managed to read what she had written.

She moved to the window, pressing her forehead against the cold glass. The wind howled outside, and for the first time since arriving in Harrowsfield, she felt the isolation of the place like a weight she couldn't escape. She had wanted to be alone. She had wanted to escape. But now, the walls of the house felt suffocating. She had come here to bury the past, not to have it resurface in ways she couldn't understand.

A thought, dark and insistent, crept into her mind: Could the house be playing tricks on her? Could the isolation be driving her mad? But no, she dismissed it quickly. She wasn't imagining this. The letter was real. The handwriting was real.

And there was only one possible conclusion. Someone was watching her. Someone had been reading her letters. Someone knew her better than she knew herself.

She picked up the letter again, staring at the cryptic message. "The past is a story you've yet to finish."

The words haunted her, echoing in her head. Was this some kind of game? A joke? No. It couldn't be. This wasn't just about someone reading her letters. This was something more. Something deeper.

Alex walked back to the table, feeling a strange mix of fear and curiosity. She opened the drawer and pulled out the letter she had written to her mother, the letter that was still raw with emotion. Then, with a sense of dread, she looked at the other letters she had written to her past—her friends, her father, her ex-lovers.

Each letter was a confession. Each one was a piece of herself she had never shared with anyone. But now, it felt as though someone else had read them. Someone who knew things she had never dared to admit.

Her hand trembled as she placed the letter to her mother back in the drawer. She couldn't stop thinking about the cryptic words: *Will you write it?*

The past was a story, she realized. And now, someone wanted her to finish it. But why? What did that mean? What did this person want from her?

The unease in her stomach grew heavier, the sense of dread that had settled over her now consuming her thoughts. She had never believed in things like fate or destiny. She had always believed that she was the one who controlled her path, her future. But now, it felt like the path was already laid out before her. Like someone else was writing her story—and she was just a character in it.

The room felt colder now, the air thick with uncertainty. She couldn't shake the feeling that someone, somewhere, was watching her every move. Someone who knew everything about her, who knew the things she hadn't even said aloud.

Alex stepped back from the table, her mind swirling with questions she couldn't answer. The letter. The message. It all felt too much.

She was no longer sure of what was real.

8

Chapter 7: Revisiting the Past

The town of Harrowsfield, with its sleepy streets and quiet corners, had become Alex's sanctuary. It was the place where she could try to rebuild herself, piece by piece, away from the remnants of her old life. Yet, no matter how much she tried to escape, the past always found a way to seep in, creeping up like a shadow, impossible to outrun.

Her mornings had become a steady routine—writing, sorting through memories, and trying to ignore the strange occurrences that seemed to follow her. The letters had become a release, a way to give voice to all the things she had never said. But each time she wrote, a new unease settled in her chest. The idea that someone, somewhere, might be reading them only made things more complicated. The cryptic letter from *The Correspondent* still hung heavily in her thoughts, its message haunting her in the stillness of the night.

Today, she found herself back at the table again, the pen resting in her hand, staring at the blank page in front of her. There was one more letter she had to write, one more person she had never truly been able to speak to. One more person who still lingered in the corners of her heart, unaddressed, unfinished.

Her former lover, Caleb.

She hadn't thought about him in years—not really. But something had shifted in the last few days, some unspoken need to confront the pieces of her life that had been left unresolved. She had tried to bury the guilt she felt about their relationship, tried to convince herself that it was better that it ended. But the truth was, she had never fully understood why it fell apart. And now, the weight of that uncertainty was unbearable.

With a deep breath, she began to write.

> *Dear Caleb,*
>
> *I've spent so many years trying to forget, but the truth is, I never really have. I thought if I just let time pass, I could leave everything behind. But I can't. There's too much between us, too much unsaid, and I can't ignore it anymore.*
>
> *I never told you how much I needed you. How much I relied on you to be the person I couldn't be for myself. And when you left, I didn't know how to pick up the pieces. I tried to move on, to pretend it didn't matter, but it did. It still does.*
>
> *I was scared, Caleb. I was scared to love, to let myself be loved. And I'm sorry for that. I pushed you away when you were the one person who could have helped me heal. I don't expect anything from you now. I just need you to know that I regret how things ended, and I regret that I never told you how much you meant to me.*

Alex paused, staring at the words she had written. The guilt still felt heavy in her chest, like a stone lodged deep in her heart. The relationship with Caleb had been one of the most meaningful of her life, yet she had let it slip away in fear. She hadn't been ready to let herself love, to trust someone else. And now, the echo of that regret lingered like a constant ache.

The letter wasn't enough. It would never be enough. But it was all she had. She folded the paper carefully and set it aside with the others, unsure whether she would ever send it, or if it was just another exercise in catharsis. Another letter to a past she couldn't escape.

The day dragged on slowly, as it always did, with the quiet rhythm of life in Harrowsfield settling around her. She went for a walk into town, the small streets winding through the heart of the village. There was a market today—something she had almost forgotten about. The vendors were set up along the square, their stalls filled with fresh produce, homemade goods, and trinkets. It was a welcome distraction, a chance to leave the house and forget about the letters for a while.

As she wandered through the market, looking at the various items on display, Alex couldn't shake the feeling that something was about to change. A vague sense of anticipation hung in the air, but she couldn't put her finger on it. The quiet of the town, the stillness she had come to appreciate, felt suddenly unfamiliar.

And then she saw him.

It was as if the world had stopped for a moment. Caleb stood by a stall, his back to her, examining a basket of apples. She froze. Her heart skipped a beat. She hadn't seen him in years. Not since they had parted ways in such a quiet, unspoken way. The last time she had heard from him, he had moved across the country, cutting off all contact. The relationship had ended, but it had never truly ended for her. It had always felt like an unfinished chapter.

Her mind raced, but her body didn't move. She wanted to turn and walk away, to pretend she hadn't seen him, to keep her distance like she had been doing for so long. But instead, she took a hesitant step forward, her feet carrying her toward him, as though drawn by some force beyond her control.

Caleb turned, his eyes catching hers for the briefest of moments. He didn't seem surprised to see her, though Alex couldn't tell if that was because he recognized her or if it was just a reflex. His features had softened with time, the sharp edges of youth replaced with the quiet maturity of someone who had lived a little longer. He looked different—more settled, somehow. But he was still Caleb. Still the person who had once meant everything to her.

For a moment, they stood there, caught in an awkward silence. Neither of them spoke, but the weight of the years between them was palpable. There was so much left unsaid, so many things Alex had wished she could ask, but the words seemed to be stuck in her throat.

Finally, Caleb spoke. His voice was low, but the familiarity of it wrapped around Alex like a blanket.

"Alex... I didn't expect to see you here," he said, his eyes soft but guarded. "How have you been?"

For a second, Alex wasn't sure how to respond. The last time she had seen him, she hadn't been ready to face the things she had been running from. She hadn't been ready to confront the way she had pushed him away. And now, standing in front of him, it felt like nothing had changed, yet everything had changed.

"I've been... okay," she said, her voice surprisingly steady. "I'm just here for a bit of peace, I guess. Trying to... sort things out."

Caleb nodded, his gaze lingering on her for a moment longer than necessary. "Yeah," he said, a small smile tugging at his lips. "I get that."

The moment stretched between them, fragile and tense. And then, as if the air had been suddenly thickened with the weight of the past, Alex felt it—a jolt, an odd sense of déjà vu. This moment, standing here, talking to Caleb, it felt familiar. Like they had already lived this moment, already shared this conversation, this awkward pause. But how?

She shook it off, telling herself it was just the strange feeling of running into someone from the past. But something about it felt wrong. Too strange. Like it wasn't the first time.

The silence grew heavier, and Alex felt the need to say something, to break the spell before it became too suffocating.

"Well," she said, clearing her throat, "It was... good to see you. Really. I should go, though."

Caleb nodded again, but there was something in his eyes that made Alex pause. "Yeah, take care of yourself, Alex," he said softly. "Maybe... we'll see each other again, sometime."

Alex smiled faintly, her heart heavy. She turned and walked away, but the odd sense of familiarity followed her, as though she were walking through a dream, a moment that had already passed.

As she left the market behind, Alex couldn't shake the feeling that she had already lived this day. Seen this person, spoken these words. It was a déjà vu that made her skin crawl.

And yet, she couldn't tell if it was a trick of her mind—or if something deeper was at play.

9

Chapter 8: The Mystery Deepens

The encounter with Caleb haunted Alex long after she left the market. The feeling of déjà vu—the sensation that she had already lived this moment—stuck with her, gnawing at her mind like a splinter she couldn't remove. She kept replaying the conversation, the way his eyes had looked at her, the way the words had flowed, as though they had both spoken this dialogue before.

But how?

She had barely seen Caleb in years, and yet their meeting felt like something rehearsed. Something familiar, as though the fabric of time itself had been stretched and bent to allow this reunion to happen again, like an old memory being replayed in real-time. It unsettled her to no end, and the questions piled up faster than she could sort through them.

Am I losing my mind?

It was the only explanation that seemed to make sense. But Alex was not one to easily accept uncertainty. She needed answers. She needed to understand what was happening, what was causing her to feel like she was living in some kind of distorted version of reality.

The strange occurrences had been escalating over the past few weeks—moving objects, letters appearing when they shouldn't, phone calls with cryptic messages. She had tried to brush it all off as coincidence, or maybe her mind playing tricks on her. But now, after meeting Caleb, after feeling the weight of that familiar, impossible encounter, she couldn't ignore the truth anymore: Something was happening. Something beyond her understanding.

That's when the idea hit her.

She needed to understand memory. She needed to understand how perception worked, how the brain could distort and manipulate what we thought we knew to be true. She had always been curious about the workings of the human mind, about how we could convince ourselves of one thing, even when the facts didn't match up. It was the perfect way to begin her search for answers.

So, the next day, she made her way to the small library in the center of town, a building that seemed frozen in time, tucked between two aging storefronts. The exterior of the library was simple, unassuming—a single story with tall windows that let in natural light. The smell of old books filled the air as Alex stepped inside, the familiar scent grounding her, offering a strange comfort in the midst of the chaos swirling around her.

It was quiet, the kind of silence that felt like it had been preserved for centuries, untouched by the outside world. The library was mostly empty, save for a few people sitting at tables, buried in their own worlds of books and research. Alex made her way through the aisles, her fingers brushing against the spines of books as she searched for something that could help her understand the strange disorienting feeling that had taken hold of her life.

She wasn't sure what exactly she was looking for, but she knew it had something to do with memory. Something about how memories could shift, change, or even fade away. She wasn't sure if it was the letters, the strange occurrences, or the voice of *The Correspondent* that had made her question everything she thought she knew, but there was one thing she was sure of: The past wasn't what it seemed.

As she walked deeper into the library, a dusty book on a high shelf caught her attention. It stood out, as though it were waiting for her to find it. The title was old, the letters yellowed with age: *Memory Manipulation: The Art of Shaping Reality Through Perception.*

Alex pulled it down from the shelf, her heart racing slightly as she flipped through the pages. The book was filled with theories, experiments, and case studies on how memory could be altered, how perceptions could be molded into something new. Some of the concepts were abstract, philosophical even, but others were more grounded—practical ways in which the human mind could be influenced, manipulated, and rewired.

Her eyes skimmed over the text, hungry for any clue that could explain what she was experiencing. The author of the book discussed how memory is not a static entity, but a fluid one—something that could be reshaped through suggestion, repetition, and, most importantly, by the way we write and think about our past.

Could this be it? Alex thought, her fingers trembling slightly as she turned the page. *Could I be rewriting my own history with these letters?*

The more she read, the more the theory began to resonate with her. The book discussed how, through writing and self-reflection, a person could rewrite the narrative of their life, their identity, and their memories. The concept was unsettling but also strangely compelling. If she was really manipulating her memories, if she was unknowingly shaping her own reality by writing to people from her past, then maybe she was the one causing the strange shifts.

Maybe the changes weren't random. Maybe they were the result of her own subconscious mind at work, reshaping the world around her as she confronted the past. The pictures that moved, the letters that appeared—could they all be part of a narrative she was unknowingly crafting?

The idea made her head spin. Was she losing touch with reality? Was she making these things happen without even realizing it? Or was someone else—*The Correspondent*—manipulating her from the outside?

The thought of someone else being involved, controlling the narrative, made her blood run cold. But the idea that she could be in control, that she had been shaping her own reality all along, was even more terrifying. If that were true, if she had the power to rewrite her past and the world around her, what else could she change? What else had she already changed without knowing it?

She took the book to one of the small tables in the library and continued to read, her mind racing as she absorbed the information. The more she learned, the less certain she became of what was happening. The lines between past and present were blurring, shifting like sand beneath her feet. She didn't know if she was losing her mind, or if she had somehow become the architect of her own reality.

Hours passed without Alex noticing. She barely even registered the passage of time, too absorbed in the words in front of her. But as the sun began to set and the library started to empty, she closed the book, the weight of the information sinking in.

The more she thought about it, the more her thoughts turned inward. Could she really trust her own memories? Could she trust what she was seeing, hearing, or feeling?

She gathered the book and stood up, feeling disoriented as she made her way to the front desk to check out. The librarian smiled at her, but the gesture felt distant, as though the world around her was shifting once more, warping and rearranging itself in ways she couldn't control.

When she stepped out of the library and into the fading light of the evening, everything felt different. The streets of Harrowsfield were quieter than usual, the shadows longer, and the air heavier with the weight of unspoken truths.

Alex couldn't shake the feeling that something was wrong. She wasn't sure if it was the book, the strange occurrences, or *The Correspondent*, but she felt as though the ground beneath her was starting to crack, just a little. The past, the present, and the future—were they really separate? Or was it all one big, tangled story that she had the power to rewrite?

The more she tried to understand it, the more she realized she couldn't tell what was real anymore.

All she knew was this: The past wasn't finished. And neither was she.

10

Chapter 9: The False Memory

The days blurred together in Harrowsfield, each one melting into the next with a quiet, almost hypnotic rhythm. Alex spent her time writing more letters, delving into the past with the hopes that facing it head-on would bring her the clarity she so desperately craved. She had written to her family, her ex-lovers, and even old friends who had faded from her life. Each letter felt like an attempt to heal, to make peace with the things she had lost.

But there was one person she hadn't yet written to. One person who had shaped her more than anyone else.

Her old mentor, Thomas Caldwell.

Thomas had been a guiding light during Alex's early career. A professor she had admired deeply, someone whose wisdom and encouragement had driven her to pursue a career in journalism. He had believed in her when no one else did, pushing her to be better, to take risks, to see the world with a critical eye.

But when he died suddenly, unexpectedly, it had left a hole in her life. Alex had never properly processed the loss. She had been too busy with the demands of her career, the chaos of her personal life, and the overwhelming grief that had followed. She had never taken the time to reflect on what he meant to her, to truly acknowledge the influence he had had on her life.

And now, here she was, in this quiet, empty house, finally able to write the things she had never said.

The pen hovered over the paper, the words coming slower than usual. But she had to try. She had to confront the feelings of inadequacy, the self-doubt that had plagued her ever since his death. She had never been able to measure up to the person he had seen in her. She had always felt like a failure, like she had let him down.

> *Dear Thomas,*
>
> *I don't know why I'm writing to you. Maybe it's because I've spent so much time pretending that I've moved on from your death, that I've found a way to carry on without confronting the weight of it. But the truth is, I've never really let go. Not of you, and not of the lessons you taught me.*
>
> *You were always the one who believed in me. You pushed me to reach for more than I thought I could achieve. You saw something in me that I couldn't see in myself. But now, years later, I find myself wondering if I've done anything worthy of that belief. I've spent so much time questioning myself, questioning whether I'm truly cut out for this, whether I've ever been good enough. You taught me to push past my doubts, but I haven't been able to shake them. I don't know if I've failed you, or if I've failed myself.*
>
> *I wish I could tell you how much you meant to me, how much I owe to you. But I never said it before, and now it's too late. I should have told you that you were more than just a mentor. You were a guide. A father figure when I needed one most. And I'm sorry for not telling you that. I'm sorry for not being the person you believed I could be.*

Alex stopped, the weight of the words pressing down on her. The guilt, the regret—it was all so overwhelming. She had let him down. She had let herself down. She had always been afraid of failing, and now, as she looked back on her life, it felt like that fear had defined her every decision.

She folded the letter carefully, setting it aside with the others. It wasn't perfect, but it was something. It was a release, even if it couldn't bring Thomas back. She needed to let go of the weight of her own expectations, the image of herself that she had tried to uphold. It was time to accept that she hadn't been able to live up to everything he had hoped for her.

But as she sat there, her thoughts swirling with the mess of emotions the letter had dredged up, something caught her eye. It was an email notification, flashing at the corner of her screen.

She clicked on it without thinking, half-expecting it to be another junk message, another piece of the clutter that filled her inbox. But as the email opened, her breath caught in her throat.

It was from Thomas.

The subject line was simple: *For Alex.*

She stared at the screen for a long moment, not quite sure if she was seeing things correctly. Thomas had been dead for years. This email shouldn't be here. It couldn't be here.

But there it was, sitting in her inbox, a message that she knew couldn't be real.

She clicked it open.

> *Dear Alex,*
>
> *I've been thinking about you a lot lately. I know you've struggled with self-doubt, with whether you've done enough, whether you've made the right choices. You've always been harder on yourself than anyone else could ever be, and I know that's kept you from*

> *reaching your full potential. But I want you to know that you've already accomplished more than you think. You've always been capable of greatness, even if you don't see it in yourself. I'm proud of you. Always will be.*
>
> *I hope you find the courage to keep going, to push past the doubts and the fears that are holding you back. And remember—failure is not the end. It's just another part of the story you're writing. Keep writing it, Alex. You have more to say than you realize.*

The words on the screen blurred before her eyes as she read them again, her heart pounding in her chest. This was impossible. Thomas was dead. There was no way he could have sent this email.

But there it was, as clear as day. It was exactly the same as the letter she had just written. The same words. The same sentiments. She had written to him, pouring out all her feelings of inadequacy and guilt, and now, this email was answering her questions, echoing the very thoughts she had put to paper.

Her hands shook as she sat back in her chair, her mind spinning. It couldn't be real. It couldn't be happening. How could it be?

But as she stared at the screen, the questions began to form, one after the other, like pieces of a puzzle she couldn't solve. Had someone accessed her computer? Had someone sent this message pretending to be Thomas? Or was it possible—just possible—that she had somehow written this email herself, in some way she couldn't remember?

The lines between memory and reality began to blur. Her mind raced, struggling to make sense of it all. Had she been writing this email without realizing it? Was she the one responsible for this strange message?

She looked at the email again, the words beginning to feel like a mockery, a cruel reflection of everything she had been writing. *Failure is not the end. It's just another part of the story you're writing.*

It was like Thomas had been speaking to her from beyond the grave, telling her exactly what she needed to hear. But she couldn't make sense of it. Could this be another manifestation of the strange things happening around her? Or was she truly losing touch with her own reality?

The room felt colder now, the shadows lengthening as the evening drew near. Alex stared at the screen, her pulse racing. Nothing made sense. And yet, in the pit of her stomach, she knew one thing for sure: she wasn't just writing letters to the past anymore. She was rewriting everything.

And she didn't know how to stop.

11

Chapter 10: Unanswered Letters

The morning was still, the air heavy with an unspoken tension. Alex sat at the table, the house quiet around her. Her fingers traced the edges of the letter she had just opened. It wasn't hers. Not one of her letters, not something she had written to herself or anyone else. This letter came from someone else, someone she hadn't thought about in years.

Tom.

Alex could hardly remember the last time she had heard from him. It had been years, long before she left the city for Harrowsfield. Tom had been one of her closest friends in college, someone she had confided in, laughed with, and even loved in a way that was never quite defined. Their friendship had been close, too close in some ways, but something had happened—something unsaid—that caused them to drift apart. Life had pulled them in different directions, and eventually, she just stopped hearing from him. They hadn't spoken since.

The letter had arrived early that morning, slipped under the door like any other piece of mail. But the moment Alex saw the handwriting on the envelope, she froze. It was his. The same familiar scrawl that she hadn't seen in years. It made her stomach drop, as if something had shifted, something she couldn't quite understand.

How was this possible? Tom was dead.

Alex's mind raced, trying to make sense of the situation. Tom had died in a car accident five years ago. She had been there, at the funeral, watching his family mourn, standing among friends who had also lost him. She had said her goodbye, along with everyone else, and accepted the finality of it. Tom was gone.

And yet, here she was, holding a letter from him.

Her hands trembled as she unfolded the paper, the words on the page staring back at her, just as clear as if they had been written yesterday.

> *Dear Alex,*
>
> *I know this is going to sound strange, but I've been thinking about you a lot lately. More than I ever thought I would. I know we didn't end things on the best note, and I've always regretted that. I should have reached out to you, should have tried harder to fix things before it was too late. But I didn't. And now it feels like the distance between us is insurmountable.*
>
> *But that's not what I'm writing to you about. I need you to know something. You've always carried this weight around, this belief that you haven't done enough, that you haven't been enough. But that's not true. You've done more than I could ever have asked of you. I hope you realize that before it's too late.*
>
> *I've watched you struggle, Alex. I've seen the pain you've carried, the regret that weighs you down. You've always been too hard on yourself. You never deserved the hurt you've been through. I can't explain why I'm writing this, but I need you to hear it from me, even if it's too late: You were never the problem. You never failed.*

The words on the page seemed to pulse in the air around her, as though they had some kind of weight, some kind of presence she couldn't quite grasp. The letter was filled with things only Tom would know—things no one else had ever seen. The guilt she carried from their broken friendship. The way she had blamed herself for everything that went wrong. The pain of never having truly made amends.

But how could Tom know this? How could he know what had been buried so deeply in her heart, the things she had never told anyone? He couldn't. He was gone.

Alex stared at the letter, a deep sense of dread washing over her. This couldn't be real. It couldn't be happening. She had come to terms with the fact that Tom was gone, that their friendship had ended, that she had no more chances to make things right. And yet, here it was. A letter from someone who was supposed to be lost forever.

Her breath quickened as she tried to steady herself. She looked around the room, as though the walls themselves might offer an explanation. She couldn't make sense of it. The letter was real, and yet everything about it felt impossible.

Her mind flickered back to the strange things she had been noticing in the house—the moving picture, the misplaced heirloom, the letter from her mother that had mirrored her own words. It was as though the past wasn't staying in the past anymore. It was coming back, manifesting in ways she couldn't control.

She reread the letter, her hands still shaking. The last few lines echoed in her mind, resonating with a sense of finality she hadn't expected.

I hope you realize that before it's too late.

Before it's too late. Those words lingered in her thoughts, gnawing at her. What did that mean? What was she supposed to realize? What was she running out of time for? And why had Tom, of all people, chosen now to send this message? Why now?

There was a growing unease in her chest, a suspicion that something deeper was happening. She wasn't just writing letters anymore. The letters were becoming real. They weren't just reflections of her thoughts and feelings—they were tangible. They were reaching back to her from the past. They were shifting reality itself.

Alex stood up suddenly, her chair scraping against the floor as she paced the room. She felt like she was suffocating, the walls closing in around her. The past had always been something she could look back on, something she could reflect on and leave behind. But now? Now the past was bleeding into the present, rearranging itself in ways she couldn't understand.

She ran her fingers through her hair, the letter still clutched in her hand. The dread inside her was growing, pushing her toward a dark realization she wasn't ready to face: *Was she rewriting the past?*

It didn't feel like she was in control anymore. It felt like something was guiding her, pushing her to confront things she wasn't ready to confront. She had written these letters, sure. But they were no longer just letters. They were becoming a force she couldn't contain.

And what if the force wasn't just hers? What if it was something else entirely?

The question echoed in her mind as she looked down at the letter from Tom, still unfolding in her hands. This wasn't just memory. This wasn't just reflection. The things she had written, the things she had left behind, were coming back. And now, they were changing everything.

Alex sank down onto the couch, the letter still in her hands, her mind spinning. She wasn't sure what was real anymore. But one thing was clear—this wasn't just about the past anymore. It was about something far bigger than she could have ever imagined.

And she was running out of time to understand it.

12

Chapter 11: The Turning Point

The evening was heavy with an unshakable sense of dread. Alex sat at the small desk in the corner of the room, the pale light of the lamp casting long shadows on the walls. She hadn't slept properly in days, her mind too consumed by the strange events that had unfolded over the past weeks. The letters, the cryptic messages, the sense of reality slipping between her fingers — it was all becoming too much.

She couldn't ignore it anymore. She couldn't pretend she wasn't part of something larger, something she didn't understand. The letters had stopped feeling like simple acts of catharsis; they felt like something more. Something dangerous.

The letter from Tom had been the final straw. How could he have written to her? How could a dead man send a letter from beyond the grave? And that voice on the phone, the cryptic messages, the way objects moved without explanation — it all pointed to one inescapable conclusion: something, or someone, was pulling the strings.

And then there was *The Correspondent.*

This mysterious figure had been lurking in the background of Alex's writing from the very beginning. First, a letter with words that mirrored her own. Then, the haunting question on the phone: *Did you ever wonder if writing could change the past?*

Now, Alex was certain. *The Correspondent* wasn't just someone else. They were part of her story. Part of her reality. But who were they, really? And how had they come to control the world she thought she understood?

She had to know. She had to confront this shadow that had been guiding her, influencing her every step.

I'm not crazy, Alex thought. *I'm not imagining this.*

Her hand hovered over the page, trembling slightly. She couldn't deny it any longer. This wasn't just about writing letters to the past. She had become part of the story itself. But she had to know the truth.

She picked up the pen.

> *Dear Correspondent,*
>
> *I've been writing these letters, pouring my thoughts and regrets into them, and for what? What am I doing? Why is this happening? I've been trying to understand, trying to figure out what's real and what isn't. But I can't. Every day, things change around me in ways I don't understand, and every time I write to the past, something shifts. Something I can't control.*
>
> *So I'm asking you now: Who are you? What is this? Why have you been guiding me through this, leading me to rewrite my own history? I need to know.*

Alex set the pen down, staring at the words she had written. She had hoped for answers, but what would the Correspondent even say? Could they give her the clarity she so desperately needed? Or would they only add to the confusion?

She folded the letter and placed it in the drawer with the others, a sense of finality settling in her chest. She was ready to face whatever came next. She had to be.

The silence of the room felt oppressive as she waited. Her thoughts raced, each unanswered question digging deeper into her mind. *Who am I really?* she wondered. *Am I in control? Or is it something—someone—else pulling the strings?*

She leaned back in the chair, staring out the window into the darkened night. The wind howled outside, but inside, the house was still. Too still. The weight of everything that had happened pressed down on her shoulders, and she couldn't shake the feeling that something was about to shift.

The minutes passed in silence. Her eyes drifted to the table, where the stack of letters sat. Letters to her mother, to her friends, to her ex-lovers. They had all been part of the puzzle, part of the story she was trying to tell. But now, she was beginning to wonder if the story had already been written. If she was just a character in someone else's narrative.

And then, as if on cue, the phone buzzed.

Alex hesitated for a moment, staring at the screen. An unknown number. She had been avoiding these calls, not wanting to hear whatever cryptic message awaited her on the other end. But tonight, something was different. The sense of dread that had been gnawing at her since she received that first letter had only grown stronger. She had to know. She had to hear it.

She answered the call, her breath catching in her throat.

"Hello?" she said, her voice unsteady.

The voice on the other end was familiar, yet foreign. The same voice that had haunted her from the very beginning. The one that had asked her if writing could change the past.

"Did you write the letter, Alex?" the voice asked, low and measured. "Did you write the truth?"

Alex's heart hammered in her chest. "What do you want from me?"

There was a pause, a moment of stillness before the voice spoke again, its tone colder now.

"You are the Correspondent."

Alex's breath caught. The words hung in the air, suspended between them. "What does that mean?"

"It means you are not just writing letters," the voice continued, "You are rewriting your own reality. Every word you write, every memory you relive, is bending the world around you. The past, the present, the future — it all bends to your will, Alex. And you've only begun to see the extent of your power."

Alex's mind reeled. *I'm rewriting my reality?* It felt impossible. But the more she thought about it, the more it made sense. The letters, the strange occurrences, the way the world seemed to shift around her... she had been writing her own story, all along. But how? Why?

The voice spoke again, this time more urgently. "You have the power to change everything, Alex. But with that power comes a price. The more you rewrite, the more you lose. The more you lose touch with what is real. And if you continue, there may be no turning back."

The line went dead.

Alex sat there, stunned, the phone still pressed to her ear. The words hung in the air, the weight of them sinking in. *You are the Correspondent.* The world bends to your will.

She felt as if the ground beneath her was crumbling, the walls of reality cracking open. She wasn't just writing letters anymore. She was rewriting her life. She was changing the very fabric of her existence.

But what did that mean for her future? For the world around her?

As the silence pressed in around her, Alex realized that everything she had known, everything she thought was true, had just shattered. She had no control over this. She didn't know how deep the rabbit hole went, but she knew one thing for sure: she had only just begun to unravel it.

And she wasn't sure if she could stop now.

13

Chapter 12: A Visitor from the Past

The knock at the door came just as the evening shadows began to lengthen, the sun slipping below the horizon and casting a dusky blue over the cottage. Alex had been sitting at the table, staring at the stack of letters she had written, the weight of *The Correspondent's* words still heavy in her mind. The world was bending to her will. She had begun to see it clearly now, the threads of reality she had been pulling, the strange distortions that were becoming harder and harder to ignore.

She had always been a woman of logic, of control, but now that seemed to be slipping through her fingers, as if the very fabric of reality was becoming a fog she couldn't quite clear. Her fingers trembled as she reached for the cup of tea that had long gone cold, trying to ground herself in the familiar routine of the quiet house. But the thought of rewriting her own reality kept creeping back, like a whisper at the edge of her thoughts.

Then came the knock.

It was soft at first, a tentative tap, and Alex felt her stomach twist. She hadn't expected visitors. The town was too small, too quiet for anyone to come calling at her door without reason. She got up slowly, heart pounding, as her feet moved almost on their own toward the door.

When she opened it, her breath caught.

Standing on her doorstep was Jordan.

Her mind went blank for a moment, the world tilting at the edges. She blinked, wondering if this was some kind of mirage, a hallucination brought on by the strange twists in her mind. Jordan stood there, her expression a mix of confusion and something else — a recognition, a familiarity that didn't feel quite right.

It had been years since Alex had last seen her. A decade, maybe longer. Their falling out had been sharp, unresolved, like a door slamming shut between them. But here Jordan was, standing on Alex's doorstep, looking just as she had the last time Alex saw her — only older, of course, her eyes a little softer, a little more guarded.

"Jordan?" Alex's voice was barely a whisper, as if saying the name would shatter the fragile reality she was clinging to. "What are you doing here?"

Jordan took a step forward, a small smile on her face that didn't quite reach her eyes. "I was hoping I'd find you here." She paused, glancing around the empty space behind Alex. "I've been looking for you for years, Alex. Ever since we lost touch."

Alex's heart raced as she stepped back, letting Jordan enter. The warmth of her presence felt alien, like a memory resurrected from the dead. She had spent years trying to forget, trying to bury the hurt, but now here she was, standing in front of her, as if time had never passed at all.

"I don't understand," Alex said, still in a daze. "How did you find me? I— I've been living here for months. I haven't talked to anyone from the old life."

"I know," Jordan said, her voice low. "I didn't know where you were at first. I didn't even know if you were still around. But then I started to get these strange signs. These feelings that kept pulling me in this direction. I didn't understand it at first, but something told me that I needed to come here. To find you."

Alex swallowed hard, her pulse thumping in her ears. "What are you talking about? How is that even possible?"

Jordan's gaze shifted, her expression becoming more serious. "I don't know. But I think... I think it's tied to the letters, Alex. I've been trying to contact you. But it wasn't until recently that I started getting these... messages. These flashes of you. Of us. Of things we talked about. Things we never even said aloud. I don't know how to explain it, but I've been following the feeling. The pull. And it led me here."

Alex's chest tightened. This was too much. This was impossible. She had written to Jordan, but she had never sent the letter. How could she have? She hadn't even known where Jordan was. She had just poured her thoughts onto the paper, the words spilling out in a desperate attempt to make sense of the loss. And now, here Jordan was, standing in front of her, claiming that the letters had brought her here.

"I don't understand," Alex whispered, her voice shaking. "How could you know? I haven't sent anything. I've only written them. And even if I had... How would you know? I— I thought I was writing to the past, to things I could never change. But you're here. How?"

Jordan stepped closer, her hand gently brushing against Alex's arm, grounding her in the present. "I don't know how it happened. But I've felt it, too. Whatever it is, it's like we're connected somehow. Like these letters — your words — have been reaching across time, across space, to pull us back together."

Alex pulled away, her thoughts whirling. This couldn't be happening. She had been trying to leave the past behind, trying to erase the mistakes and regrets. But Jordan's arrival felt like the past had come crashing into the present, refusing to be ignored.

"Why are you here, really?" Alex asked, the words falling out before she could stop them. "What do you want from me?"

Jordan's expression softened, but there was something unreadable in her eyes. "I don't want anything from you, Alex. I've come because I think we need to finish what we started. I think we need to make sense of this... whatever this is. I think we need to confront what happened between us."

Alex felt a cold wave wash over her. What was happening? Was this part of the strange reality she had been unknowingly rewriting? Was this the effect of the letters, or was it something more sinister? Was Jordan really here, or was she a product of Alex's mind, another figure conjured from the past to fill the void?

"You're... you're not real," Alex whispered, her voice cracking. "You're not real. This can't be happening."

But as she said the words, she saw Jordan's face soften with recognition, the same familiar expression that had once been a comfort, now tinged with sadness.

"I am real, Alex," Jordan said quietly, her voice full of the same quiet understanding they had shared once before. "And I think... I think you need to understand something."

Alex shook her head. "No. I'm losing my mind. I have to be. You can't be here. This can't be happening."

Jordan stepped back, her eyes never leaving Alex's. "Maybe you're right. Maybe you're losing your mind. Or maybe you're just beginning to understand what's really happening. I think you've been writing your story, Alex. I think you've been rewriting your reality. And I think this —" she gestured around the room, her eyes filled with quiet understanding, "— is the result of everything you've written. Every word you've sent to the past. And now, it's coming for you."

Alex's breath caught in her throat. *Coming for me?* Was this the price? The cost of rewriting her life, of bending the world around her? She had written herself into this reality, and now, the past was demanding to be faced.

"Why now?" Alex asked, her voice barely audible. "Why are you here now?"

Jordan looked at her with a mixture of sorrow and knowing. "Because, Alex, the past doesn't stay buried. It's calling you. And you can't ignore it any longer."

As the words hung in the air, Alex felt the weight of them settle deep within her. The line between the past and present had been erased, and now there was no escaping it.

14

Chapter 13: Fractured Reality

The morning was like any other — or at least, it seemed that way at first. The sun filtered through the curtains in thin streams of light, casting long shadows across the room. Alex had woken earlier than usual, the weight of restless dreams still lingering in her mind. The house was quiet, still, almost too still, and for a moment, she thought she had imagined the events of the night before — the encounter with Jordan, the unsettling revelations. But then she remembered the letter from Tom, and the cryptic message from *The Correspondent.*

It was all real. And the reality she had been clinging to began to feel increasingly fragile.

She got up, her legs shaky as she made her way downstairs to the kitchen. She opened the door, expecting to hear the usual creak of the floorboards and the hum of the wind outside, but something felt off. The silence in the air was thicker, more pressing. Her eyes scanned the room, landing on the stack of letters on the table — her letters. All the things she had written to confront the past, to reshape the world she had left behind.

But now, as she stood in the kitchen, she wondered if it was all too late.

She took a breath, trying to steady her racing heart. Her fingers brushed the edge of her coffee mug as she lifted it to her lips, but as she took a sip, something happened — something small, almost imperceptible. The taste was wrong. It wasn't the coffee she had brewed. It tasted stale, almost like it had been sitting for hours.

She pulled the mug away from her lips, looking at it with confusion. *Hadn't I just made this?* The thought lingered in her mind, but before she could process it, a knock at the door broke her thoughts.

She didn't expect anyone. No one ever came by this far out of town. But she went to answer it anyway, half-expecting another strange occurrence, another intrusion from her past.

When she opened the door, she was greeted by the same sight she had seen before — Jordan, standing there, her face filled with an unreadable expression.

"I... I thought I saw you earlier?" Alex stammered. The words felt foreign, like she had already said them.

Jordan blinked at her, as if confused. "You didn't see me earlier," she replied slowly, "We just spoke now. Are you okay?"

Alex froze, her heart skipping a beat. She had just seen Jordan standing in front of her — in the exact same position, wearing the same clothes. But... hadn't they already spoken?

What's happening?

Her thoughts began to spin, the ground beneath her seeming to shift. This moment, this conversation — it felt like she had lived it before. The words she had just spoken, the look on Jordan's face, the small details — they were all too familiar. Alex didn't know how, but it was as if she had experienced this exact moment in time already.

The house, the room, the air — everything seemed to pulse with an odd, distorted energy. The walls closed in on her as she tried to grasp at the threads of reality. Her pulse quickened as she looked at Jordan, who stood there, watching her with a concerned look in her eyes.

"Are you feeling alright?" Jordan asked, her tone gentle. "You look...

like you've seen a ghost."

Alex swallowed, her mind a mess of confusion and dread. "I... I think I'm losing my mind."

Before Jordan could answer, Alex turned quickly, stepping back inside the house, trying to shake the feeling of déjà vu. It was happening again. She had already had this conversation, already seen Jordan standing at the door. But now, it was as if the moment had reset itself. The world had looped back, and she was reliving it.

She ran to the kitchen, trying to gather herself, trying to steady her breath. The air felt thick, too heavy, and the shadows seemed to stretch unnaturally. She could hear the familiar creak of the floorboards behind her as Jordan entered the room, just as she had moments before.

"Are you sure you're okay?" Jordan asked again, her voice filled with a quiet concern.

This time, Alex couldn't ignore it. Her mind screamed at her that something was wrong. That this wasn't happening for the first time — it was happening again.

"I... I don't know," Alex whispered. "This has happened before. I already talked to you. This conversation... it's happening again. I swear it."

Jordan's brow furrowed, and she stepped closer. "Alex, you're scaring me. We just met here. I just came to check on you."

But Alex didn't hear her anymore. The world was folding in on itself, time splintering into jagged pieces. The air around her seemed to warp, the room tilting as if she was caught in some strange version of reality that she couldn't escape.

The knocking at the door, the smell of the coffee, the conversation — it was all replaying in her mind, each moment looping like a broken record. And the more she tried to piece it together, the more everything around her felt strange, alien. The town outside, the familiar houses lining the streets — everything had begun to feel like a dream, a place she had already visited.

"Alex?" Jordan's voice pulled her back, but it only deepened the confusion. "Please, just breathe. Everything is fine."

"Is it?" Alex's voice cracked as she looked out the window, the world outside looking oddly distorted, like a reflection in cracked glass. She stepped forward, her feet unsteady, as though she were walking through a fog.

"I've been here before. This whole moment. This house. This room. It's like it's repeating itself," she said, her voice trembling. "Everything feels... wrong. Like I'm stuck in a loop."

Jordan's expression softened, but there was something unreadable in her eyes. "It's okay, Alex. You're just exhausted. You've been through a lot. You need to rest."

Alex's heart pounded in her chest. "No," she whispered. "It's not that. Something's happening. I can feel it. Time... it's breaking. It's like I'm stuck in a place where nothing's moving forward."

The feeling of time warping, of events repeating themselves, intensified. Her hands gripped the table, trying to steady herself, but everything around her seemed to tilt and shift, just out of reach. The words she had written to Jordan, the phone calls, the strange distortions in her reality — they were all converging, becoming too real to ignore.

"I'm not imagining this," Alex said aloud, her voice growing more desperate. "I can feel it. This isn't just in my head. Something is wrong. Something is changing."

Jordan stepped closer, but Alex took a step back, her breath coming in shallow gasps. The weight of everything was too much, and the world seemed to collapse in on itself.

"Alex, I'm here. Everything's going to be alright. Just breathe."

But Alex couldn't breathe. The air was thick with the disorienting feeling of time breaking. She looked around the room, feeling like she was seeing it for the first time — or had she already seen it? Had this moment already happened? She couldn't tell anymore.

"Time's looping," Alex muttered. "It's looping, and I can't escape it."

Suddenly, it hit her: The past wasn't just something she was writing. It was something that was rewriting itself around her. The more she wrote, the more the world shifted. The boundaries between what was real and what was imagined were disintegrating.

Alex staggered back, the ground beneath her feeling unstable. The lines between the past and present were bleeding together, and she was losing her grip on both.

The town — the house, the people, everything — was changing. And the more she tried to hold on, the further she fell into the fracture of reality.

15

Chapter 14: The Missing Letter

The days were beginning to blur into one long, uninterrupted stretch of confusion and dread. Alex spent more time writing, trying to make sense of everything, but with each letter, it felt like she was sinking deeper into a hole she couldn't escape. The strange occurrences were only escalating: the repeated conversations with Jordan, the sense that time itself was folding in on itself, like some distorted memory that she couldn't control.

And then, the letter appeared.

She had been sitting in the small living room, her eyes fixed on the pages of a book she couldn't seem to focus on. The silence of the cottage had become oppressive, each tick of the clock sounding like a hammer in her ears. She had tried to lose herself in the pages, tried to escape from the mounting chaos in her mind, but the words weren't enough. The more she read, the more she felt like she was suffocating, drowning in her own thoughts.

And that's when she saw it — a letter, sitting on the table in front of her.

At first, she didn't notice anything unusual. It looked just like all the other letters she had written over the past weeks. The familiar envelope, the same handwriting — it was her handwriting, the same precise script she had seen a hundred times. But there was something off about it. Something unsettling.

She reached for it, her fingers trembling as she turned it over in her hands. Her name was written on the front, just like all the others, but this one was different. She didn't remember writing it. She didn't remember sending it. She hadn't even seen it before.

Her breath caught in her throat as she slowly opened the envelope. Her heart raced, the weight of the letter feeling too heavy for something she had no memory of writing. As she unfolded the paper, she could feel her pulse quickening, an uneasy sense of dread creeping up her spine.

It was addressed to her. From her.

> *Dear Alex,*
>
> *You don't know me. But I know you. You've written so many letters to the past, to people who've left your life, trying to make sense of the things that have been lost. But you haven't looked at the one letter you've been avoiding all along: the letter to yourself.*
>
> *You've already written your future. Every step, every choice, every moment is already laid out before you. But what happens when you run out of words? What happens when there are no more letters to write?*
>
> *You think you're in control. But you're not. You're trapped in a narrative you can't escape. The words are running out, and soon, you'll be left with nothing but silence.*

You need to stop writing. Before it's too late.

The words burned in Alex's mind, each sentence a cruel echo of everything she had feared. *You've already written your future.* The letter felt like a punch to the gut, the weight of it sinking in as she tried to make sense of what she was reading. How could she have written this?

How could she have written to herself without even remembering it? It felt as though the letter had come from a place she couldn't reach, from a version of herself that she didn't recognize.

She set the letter down on the table, her fingers trembling as she stared at it, unable to process what she had just read. The handwriting was hers, but the words weren't. They were a warning, a message she didn't know how to interpret.

The room began to spin. She felt like the walls were closing in around her, the familiar space becoming strange and alien. The words from the letter reverberated in her mind, and the more she thought about it, the more it felt like she was trapped in some kind of cycle. *You're trapped in a narrative you can't escape.* Was that true? Was she writing her own future? Had she already made all the choices that would lead her to this moment?

Her breath became shallow, her pulse hammering in her ears. She stood up, pacing the room, trying to shake the feeling of being trapped. The house, the letters, the strange occurrences — it all felt like it was slipping away from her. She wasn't in control anymore. She hadn't been in control for a long time.

The past isn't finished. The future is already written. What happens when the words run out?

The idea of running out of words terrified her. If she was trapped in this story, what would happen when she reached the end? What would happen when there were no more letters to write, no more memories to revisit?

She tried to push the thoughts aside, but they wouldn't go away. The letter to herself had shattered the fragile illusion she had built. The idea that she could rewrite her life, that she had been in control all along, felt like a lie. What if everything she had written was just another part of a story that was being forced upon her? What if the world she had tried to reshape was already set in motion, and she was nothing more than a character trapped within it?

The town outside felt different now, too. It had always seemed quiet, peaceful, but now it felt suffocating. The streets she had walked a hundred times before now looked unfamiliar, distorted somehow. The faces of the people who lived here, the small-town familiarity — it all seemed like a mirage, a dream she couldn't wake up from.

Alex moved to the window, looking out at the town that had once felt like an escape, but now felt like a prison. The town, the house, the letters — it was all part of the same world. A world that she had created, but now couldn't control.

She didn't know how much longer she could keep writing, keep trying to rewrite what had already been written. The fear gnawed at her, an ever-present reminder that she might be running out of time, running out of words.

She had been trying to shape her reality, trying to escape from the past, but now it felt like the past was coming for her, closing in with every letter she wrote. The more she tried to change the story, the more she realized she was only making it worse.

The words from the letter echoed in her mind again, like a warning she couldn't ignore: *What happens when you run out of words?*

Alex didn't know the answer. But she was afraid to find out.

16

Chapter 15: The Unseen Hand

The house felt suffocating. The walls, once a comforting refuge, now pressed in on Alex from all sides, like the closing of a book whose final page was rapidly approaching. The letter she had received, the one from herself, echoed in her mind with every beat of her heart: *What happens when you run out of words?*

Alex had written to everyone — her family, her old friends, even strangers who had once played roles in her life. She had written her past, and in doing so, she had thought she could escape it. But now, the past wasn't just following her. It was consuming her. She could feel the weight of her own creation pressing down on her, like a storm gathering on the horizon.

She had to know. She had to confront *The Correspondent* — the mysterious figure who had been guiding her, manipulating her, shaping her reality from the shadows. The figure who had always been a whisper, a presence in the background of her letters. Now, she could no longer avoid the question: *Who are you?*

Her mind raced as she paced the living room, her thoughts tangled in confusion and fear. She had been trying to write her way out of the mess she had created, trying to rewrite her life, but what if that wasn't enough? What if she was only making things worse?

Her fingers gripped the edges of the table, the familiar wood cool beneath her touch. The door to the outside world was open — the wind rustling the trees, the sun beginning its descent beneath the horizon. And yet, everything felt wrong. The world outside was fading, blurring, like a dream she couldn't hold on to.

The time had come.

Taking a deep breath, Alex sat down at the table, the stack of letters in front of her. She had written to the past, to her loved ones, but she had never written to *The Correspondent.* She had never addressed the presence that had been guiding her, manipulating the very world she had tried to control. It was time to end it. Time to face what had been growing in the dark corners of her mind.

She picked up the pen, her hand shaking, but determined. She knew this would be the last letter she wrote. The last words she would try to control.

> *Dear Correspondent,*
>
> *I know you've been watching. I know you've been guiding me through these letters, twisting the world around me in ways I don't understand. But I need to know. How are you doing this? How have you been able to manipulate my reality?*
>
> *I've written about my past, my regrets, my failures. I've written about everything I've lost. But now, the world feels like it's falling apart. The more I write, the more I feel like I'm losing control. I can't run from this anymore. I need answers. I need to know what you are, what you've done to me.*
>
> *Please, tell me the truth. Who are you?*

She set the pen down, her heart pounding in her chest as she stared at the letter. The room felt colder now, as if the world itself had grown distant. She had written the words, but they didn't seem like her own. It was as though they had come from somewhere deeper, somewhere she had buried a long time ago.

She waited.

The silence stretched, thick and oppressive, and just as she was about to get up, to walk away from the letter and the madness she had created, it happened.

The air around her shifted. The world seemed to bend in on itself, the walls warping, the light from the windows flickering like a broken film reel. Alex's breath caught in her throat as the shadows in the room began to move. The space around her felt like it was collapsing, and for a split second, she feared she was losing her grip on reality.

And then, the figure appeared.

It was neither a man nor a woman, but something in between. A presence, cloaked in shadow, with no face — no features. The figure stood in the doorway, and though Alex couldn't see it clearly, she could feel it. It was like looking into a mirror that didn't reflect what was truly there. The figure was her creation, and yet it wasn't. It was the embodiment of everything she had written, everything she had feared, and everything she had tried to escape.

The voice that came from the figure was calm, steady, almost familiar, like the echo of her own thoughts.

"You've been asking who I am," it said, its tone soft, almost reassuring. "But the answer is simple: I am you, Alex."

Alex's mind reeled. "What do you mean? How is that possible? You're not real. You can't be me."

The figure stepped forward, its presence filling the room. "I am the part of you that you've hidden, the part of you that created me. The part of you that wanted to rewrite the world. The part of you that needed control. I am your subconscious, the force behind every letter you've written. The one who has been guiding you to confront the past, to shape your reality. But you haven't been writing just to make sense of your life. You've been writing to make a new world. A world where you can control the outcome."

"No," Alex breathed, shaking her head. "That's not possible. I didn't mean to... I didn't mean for any of this to happen."

The figure tilted its head, its voice growing softer. "That's what you don't understand, Alex. You *wanted* this. You created me, and with me, you've been rewriting your reality. But now, you've reached the breaking point. You've been writing yourself into this story, but the story can't go on forever. What happens when you run out of words?"

Alex stumbled back, the weight of the words sinking in. "I've been writing... this whole time?" she whispered, her voice breaking. "I've been controlling all of this? But how? How could I—"

The figure stepped closer, its shadow enveloping her like a fog. "You think you've been writing to the past, but you've been writing to the present. Every letter, every word, has changed the world around you. You created me. You wrote me into existence. And now, you've come to a point where the world can no longer bend. The story is running out of room."

Alex's breath hitched in her throat. She had been writing this all along. She had been writing *herself* into existence, shaping the reality around her with every word she put to paper. She hadn't been running from the past; she had been recreating it, giving life to the very things she feared.

"You're not just the Correspondent," Alex whispered, as the truth began to sink in. "You're me."

The figure nodded slowly, its presence growing stronger. "Yes. I am the part of you that has never been willing to accept the world as it is. But now, you must face the consequences of your creation."

Alex's mind spun as the reality around her began to warp. The walls of the cottage stretched and bent, the air crackling with the tension of what was happening. The letters, the town, the people — it was all slipping away, like sand through her fingers. She had written it all, had tried to rewrite the life she had lost. But now, there was no more room to rewrite.

"Will you let go?" the figure asked, its voice now laced with something darker. "Will you accept that the story must end, or will you continue to bend the world to your will?"

Alex's heart thundered in her chest as she took a shaky step back. The figure seemed to fill the entire room now, its presence suffocating, inescapable. She couldn't breathe, couldn't think. It was all collapsing. She had been writing, yes. She had been creating her world, but now she was trapped in it. The more she wrote, the more she lost control. The world she had crafted was consuming her.

The letters, the memories, the past — they were no longer just words on paper. They were real. And now, they were taking over.

And Alex wasn't sure if she could stop it.

17

Chapter 16: Rewriting the Past

The night had come slowly, creeping in as the quiet house seemed to settle deeper into itself. The air was thick with the weight of everything Alex had learned in the past weeks — the letters, the power she hadn't fully understood, and the confrontation with *The Correspondent.* She felt as if she had been teetering on the edge of something monumental, something she had only just begun to comprehend.

The past wasn't something you could escape. It wasn't something you could rewrite at will.

But maybe she could try.

Her fingers hovered over the paper as she sat at the kitchen table. The pen trembled in her hand, her heart heavy with the words she had never said, the apology she had never given. She hadn't written a letter to him yet, the person who haunted her thoughts like a shadow, the one who had caused the deepest wound in her life.

Her father.

She had never been able to bridge the gap between them, never been able to forgive him for the years of neglect, the words left unsaid, the absence that had defined their relationship. Her father had been a figure who loomed in the background of her life, a man she could never quite reach, never quite understand. He had abandoned her, and in doing so, he had broken something inside her that had never healed.

Alex had spent years running from that hurt. But now, sitting in the dim light of the kitchen, the letters — the words — felt like the only way to confront it. The only way to face the man who had shaped so much of who she was, even if she had spent her life trying to escape him.

The letter was harder to write than any she had written before. The words felt like stones in her chest, but she couldn't stop. She had to say it, had to let it out.

> *Dear Dad,*
>
> *I don't know where to begin. We've never been good at talking. We never were. But maybe that's why I'm writing this, because it's the only way I know how to say the things I've kept locked inside for so long.*
>
> *You've been a ghost in my life, Dad. Always there, but never really here. I've carried that ghost with me, every day, every year. I've spent so much of my life wondering what went wrong, blaming myself for things that were never my fault.*
>
> *I've tried to hate you. I've tried to move on without you, to pretend that your absence didn't matter. But it does. It always has. I don't know why you left, why you chose to walk away from everything we could have had. But I've spent years trying to fix it, trying to fill that empty space with everything else but the truth.*
>
> *I'm not writing this to ask for anything from you, Dad. I'm not writing this to fix the past, because I know it's too late for that. But I need you to know that I've spent my life trying to make peace with the fact that you're not here. I've needed you, and I've never had the courage to say it.*

> *I don't know what forgiveness looks like, or if it even matters anymore. But I need you to know that I'm tired of carrying the weight of your absence. I'm tired of pretending it doesn't hurt. I'm tired of pretending that I can fix something that's already broken.*
>
> *I don't expect anything from you. I just need to say this, even if it's too late to matter. I need to say that I'm sorry too. For everything I never understood. For everything I never said.*
>
> *I don't know what the future holds, but I want to stop running from this. I want to stop pretending that I don't need you. I'm sorry for not telling you that sooner.*

Alex set the pen down, staring at the letter in front of her. It was raw, too honest, and far too real. The words felt like a release, but they also felt like a door she couldn't close. She had said everything she had never been able to say. She had written the truth, the things she had buried deep in her heart for years.

But now that it was on paper, she felt exposed, vulnerable. She wasn't sure what would happen after she wrote it. Would it bring peace? Would it change anything?

She folded the letter carefully, setting it aside. It wasn't finished. She wasn't sure if it would ever be. But for now, it was enough.

She stood up, rubbing her eyes. The exhaustion of the last few weeks had taken its toll on her, and she needed rest. She moved toward the staircase, but before she could make it to the top, a noise stopped her dead in her tracks.

The unmistakable sound of a chair scraping against the floor.

Alex froze. She turned slowly, her pulse spiking.

The kitchen was empty, the table where she had been writing still standing as it had been. But there, sitting at the kitchen table, was her father.

He looked the same as he had in her memories — older, of course, but the same. His rough features, his worn eyes, the faint stubble on his chin. He looked at her like nothing had changed, like nothing had ever happened between them.

Alex's breath caught in her throat. She couldn't move. She couldn't speak. This couldn't be happening.

But there he was. Sitting at the table, as though nothing had ever happened, as though the years of absence, of pain, of lost time, had never existed.

"Dad?" Alex whispered, her voice breaking. "What... What are you doing here?"

Her father didn't speak at first. He just sat there, looking at her with those same tired eyes. His hands rested on the table, his posture relaxed, as though he were waiting for her to answer.

"Alex," he said, his voice a low rumble. "I've been trying to find you for years. I didn't know where you were. I didn't know how to make things right. But here I am."

The words felt like a weight, pressing against Alex's chest. Her knees buckled, and she sat down heavily in the chair across from him, the world spinning around her.

"How?" she whispered, her voice hoarse. "How are you here? I— I wrote to you. I didn't send it, but how are you here?"

Her father's gaze softened, and for the first time in years, Alex saw a flicker of something in his eyes. Regret? Sorrow? She couldn't tell.

"You wrote to me," he said quietly, "and I've been listening."

Alex's heart thudded in her chest. The letter. The words she had poured out so freely, the raw emotions she had never expressed. They were real. He had read them. And now, he was here. Sitting in front of her, as though nothing had changed.

But everything had changed.

Her father, the man who had been absent for so long, was now here — but in a way that felt impossible. This moment, this reality, was something she hadn't planned for. Something she couldn't control.

She wanted to reach for him, to ask him everything she had never dared to ask, but the words caught in her throat. The air felt thick with the weight of the past.

"I don't understand," Alex murmured, her eyes filling with tears. "I don't know what's happening. What have I done?"

Her father remained silent, and for a long time, the two of them just sat there, across from each other, caught in the stillness of a moment that felt both too real and not real enough.

Alex didn't know how this would end. She didn't know if this was the beginning of some kind of healing or the last step into something darker. But as she looked at him — her father, finally present — she couldn't escape the truth: she had rewritten her past. And now, she had to face the consequences.

18

Chapter 17: The Correspondent's Game

The weight of the letter to her father still lingered in Alex's mind as she sat at the kitchen table, her fingers tapping nervously against the empty mug in front of her. Her father's sudden appearance was still impossible to process, the reality of it too surreal, too much like a dream she couldn't wake up from. Had she really brought him back into her life? Had she somehow written him into existence?

The more Alex thought about it, the more the truth began to settle in — this wasn't just about writing letters to the past anymore. The letters had stopped being a means of catharsis. They weren't simply reflections of her regrets or unfinished conversations. They were becoming something more.

They were controlling her.

The weight of it hit her suddenly. The power she had felt while writing, the freedom she thought she had gained by rewriting the past — it had never been freedom at all. It had been a trap.

Her eyes flickered toward the stack of letters on the table, each one like a piece of her past and present woven together. But now, each letter felt like an entry in someone else's game. She hadn't been writing to herself, to the past — she had been writing a story that was already unfolding.

The realization was suffocating. *You are the Correspondent.* Those words from the shadowy figure — the one who had been guiding her, who had been influencing her every move — echoed in her mind, over and over again.

She hadn't been in control. She never had been.

The walls of the cottage suddenly felt like they were closing in on her, the air thicker, more oppressive. The house that had once been her sanctuary now felt like a cage, each corner a reminder of the reality she had unwittingly bent to her will.

Her breath grew shallow as she stood up, pacing the room, trying to think, to make sense of the spiral her life had become. The correspondence — the letters, the strange occurrences — they had all been leading her here, to this point, where she realized that she was no longer in control.

Her hands shook as she reached for the phone, but before she could dial, it buzzed in her hand. An unknown number, as it had so many times before. This time, she didn't hesitate. She answered, her voice tight.

"Hello?"

The voice on the other end was familiar, but distorted, like it had been filtered through a haze. "You've been writing, Alex," the voice said, its tone calm, almost too calm. "You've been rewriting your world. But now you're beginning to see the truth, aren't you?"

Alex's pulse quickened, a sense of dread creeping up her spine. "What do you want from me?"

The voice didn't answer immediately. When it spoke again, its words were slow, deliberate, like someone savoring the moment. "You've been writing your own story, yes. But now the game has changed. And you, Alex, are no longer the player. You are the pawn."

Alex's stomach dropped. "What do you mean? What is this?"

"You see, Alex," the voice continued, "you're trapped in a loop. You've been rewriting your past, your present, trying to fix things, trying to escape the pain, but every time you write, every time you try to change something, you lose a piece of yourself. You're losing control of the very thing you've tried to bend. The more you write, the more the world bends to *me*, to the Correspondent. And the more you try to control it, the more you slip away."

Alex's breath hitched. "No. I can't be... I can't be the pawn. I've been writing, yes, but I was trying to fix it! I was trying to make things right. I'm not doing this for you. I'm doing this for me. For my peace."

The voice chuckled softly, the sound sending chills down her spine. "You never had peace, Alex. You're only rewriting your reality to escape it. But the more you rewrite, the more you become a character in a story you don't even remember writing. And soon, there will be nothing left but the words. Nothing but the story."

The line went silent, and for a moment, Alex stood there, gripping the phone, her mind racing. *A character in a story she didn't remember writing?* What did that even mean? Was her life no longer her own? Had she been living in a reality she had crafted only to realize that it had always been someone else's design?

The thought was too much to bear.

The phone buzzed again, this time with a new message. She glanced down at it, her heart sinking as she read the words that appeared on the screen.

"You've already written your future. What happens when you run out of words? Keep writing, Alex. I'm watching."

She dropped the phone in shock, the device hitting the floor with a sharp crack. The message echoed in her mind. *Keep writing.* But why? What was the point? If she was already trapped in this narrative, what else was left to write?

A voice from the corner of the room broke through her thoughts. She hadn't heard anyone enter, but there, standing in the doorway, was *The Correspondent*. The figure she had created. The manifestation of her own subconscious, the one who had been pulling the strings all along.

But now, as the figure stepped forward, Alex realized something — it wasn't just her creation. It wasn't just a part of her mind. It had become real, standing in front of her. It was no longer a shadow in her thoughts; it was a presence she couldn't escape.

"You've been writing for so long, Alex," the figure said, its voice both soothing and terrifying. "But now the story is shifting. And you're no longer the one in control. The lines between you and the world are blurring. And soon, there will be nothing left but the words."

Alex stepped back, her mind reeling. "You've been controlling this whole time. Haven't you?"

The figure nodded slowly, its shape shifting with every movement. "Of course. But you were always part of this game. You've been writing me into existence. Every word you wrote was a piece of the story. Every time you tried to change something, you gave me more power. And now, the story is yours. But it's not the one you think it is."

Alex's legs buckled beneath her as she sank to the floor, her hands clutching her head. "What have I done?" she whispered. "What have I created?"

"You've created a world that bends to your will," the Correspondent said, stepping closer. "But every story has an end. And you're nearing yours."

The words hit her like a tidal wave, crashing over her, suffocating her. She had been writing, yes, but now she understood. She hadn't been writing her life — she had been writing her doom. The more she tried to fix things, the more she lost herself in the pages.

And now, the world was collapsing under the weight of her creation.

19

Chapter 18: The Unwritten Letter

The house was quieter than it had ever been before. The air seemed to hang thick with the weight of everything Alex had learned, everything she had realized. The walls of the cottage, once a sanctuary, now felt like the cold boundaries of a prison, trapping her inside a narrative she could no longer control.

You've created this, she thought. *You've written yourself into this story.*

The realization had come too late. She had spent so long trying to rewrite her past, to fix the mistakes, to make the wrong things right. But with each letter, with every word, she had bent the world around her in ways she didn't understand. Now, the world was closing in on her, and she was no longer sure what was real.

The Correspondent's words still echoed in her mind. *Every story has an end.* Alex had tried to run from that truth, tried to change it, but it was clear now — she was writing the end of her own story, and she was too far gone to stop it.

But there was one last thing she had to do. One last letter she needed to write — a letter to herself.

She had avoided this moment for as long as she could. Writing letters to others had been a way to deflect, a way to avoid confronting the deepest parts of herself. But now, standing in the middle of the quiet house, the truth felt unavoidable. She had to write this letter.

Alex sat down at the table, the pen heavy in her hand. The room was dimly lit, the soft glow of the lamplight casting long shadows on the floor. She glanced at the stack of letters — all the ones she had written before, each one an attempt to reconcile with her past, to make peace with the people she had lost. But this letter was different. It wasn't for anyone else. It was for her.

She closed her eyes, her heart racing, as she set the pen to paper.

> *Dear Alex,*
>
> *I don't know where to begin. Maybe because I've spent so much of my life running from this moment. Running from the things I've never wanted to face. I've spent years trying to write the perfect story — a story that makes sense, that ties up the loose ends, that explains the choices I've made. But every time I try, I end up in the same place. Stuck. And I realize now that the only thing I haven't written is the truth.*
>
> *I've been afraid for so long. Afraid of failing. Afraid of being hurt. Afraid of never being enough. And in all that fear, I've created a world I can't control. A world where I'm constantly rewriting everything to make it fit the way I want it to. But what if I can't rewrite the past? What if the things I've lost can never come back? What if the things I've done can't be undone?*
>
> *I don't know how to fix everything. I don't know how to make all of this okay. But I want to. I want to believe that it's still possible. That the choices I've made, the ones that haunt me, the ones I can't take back, can still lead to something good. But I'm scared. I'm scared that I'll keep running. That I'll keep writing and rewriting until there's nothing left of me but words.*

> *Maybe I don't have to fix everything. Maybe I just need to stop writing for a moment and face what's real. Maybe the truth isn't something I can change, but something I have to accept. And maybe, just maybe, that's where I'll find peace.*

She paused, her hand shaking as she set the pen down. The letter was raw, painful, a confession she had never thought she would make. But as she read the words again, she felt something shift inside her. The heaviness that had been sitting on her chest for so long seemed to ease, just a little.

She folded the letter, carefully, and set it aside on the table. This time, she didn't need to send it. This was the letter that would finally give her the clarity she had been seeking. The last piece of the puzzle she had been trying to solve for so long.

She didn't want to think about it anymore. She wanted to go to bed, sleep, and wake up to a world that felt real again. But when she woke up the next morning, she found something she wasn't prepared for.

The letter was gone.

She blinked, her heart stopping in her chest as she looked at the empty space where the folded paper had been. It wasn't on the table. It wasn't anywhere.

Her breath caught as she stood up, the blood draining from her face. She checked the drawers, the other letters, the floor — anywhere she could think of. But it was nowhere. Her mind raced. Had she imagined it? Had she written it in her sleep?

But as her pulse quickened, she looked outside the window, and that's when it hit her.

The town wasn't the same.

It looked... different.

The streets she had walked a hundred times before, the houses that had always felt familiar — they were now unrecognizable. They were the same, and yet not. It was as if the town had shifted, subtly, like a picture that had been hung crookedly on the wall and had only now settled into place. The air was colder. The streets felt emptier. And the people — the people felt like strangers.

But it wasn't just the town. It was her life. It was her reality.

She stepped outside, feeling the change like a weight pressing against her chest. Her footsteps felt heavier as she moved through the familiar streets, but nothing felt familiar anymore.

When she reached the corner of the street, she saw something that made her blood run cold. The familiar café she used to visit — the one where she had spent so many mornings, lost in her thoughts — was now a new, unfamiliar place. The sign read *"Morris & Co."* in bold, modern letters. It wasn't the same place she remembered. It couldn't be.

Alex turned quickly, her mind spinning as she tried to make sense of it all. The letter had disappeared. The town had changed. And the most terrifying thought crossed her mind — *Was this a reality I had written, or had I rewritten myself into a life I didn't even recognize anymore?*

She turned back toward the house, her heart pounding as she realized the truth: the letter had been a turning point. By writing to herself, she had crossed a line. She had rewritten her past in ways that had warped her present.

And now, she was standing in a reality where the world no longer felt like her own.

20

Chapter 19: The Price of Control

The house no longer felt like a home. It was as if it had shifted beneath Alex's feet, taking on a strange, unwelcoming quality. The walls, which had once held the echoes of her past, now seemed hollow. The silence was overwhelming, not peaceful but suffocating, pressing in from every direction. Alex could no longer find solace in the spaces she had once found comfort. The letters, the words, the revisions — they had brought her nothing but confusion and pain.

The morning had started like any other, but by mid-day, Alex was already feeling the ground beneath her wobble, as if the world itself had become unsteady. It wasn't just the disorienting changes to the town, or the strange way her past kept bleeding into her present. Time itself felt... off. It felt like it was stretching and warping, slipping through her fingers like water.

She stared at the clock on the wall. The hands were moving erratically, speeding up and slowing down in intervals, as if they were trying to pull her into some other reality, one where the rules didn't apply. The minutes blurred together. She couldn't remember if she had been sitting there for an hour or a day.

She closed her eyes, trying to steady her breathing. But when she opened them again, the room had shifted. The air was different, colder, heavier.

The letters. They were always there, stacked neatly on the table, taunting her, as if they held the answers to everything — and yet nothing at all. Each one was a page in a story she could never finish, a story she had tried to rewrite over and over, but no matter how many times she turned the pages, the ending was always the same.

And the strangest part? Every letter she had written, every word she had poured out onto paper, seemed to ripple through time, distorting her memories. What was real? What was her past? What was the truth?

Alex stood up abruptly, the chair scraping against the floor. The feeling of vertigo crept up on her, as though she were losing her grip on everything she knew. The air felt thicker now, almost oppressive, as if the very atmosphere were conspiring against her. She stumbled toward the door, but when she reached for the handle, her hand froze.

Something was wrong.

She turned back toward the kitchen, where the stack of letters still sat. But when she looked at them, the ink seemed to blur, the words shifting and changing before her eyes. *No*, she thought, desperately trying to make sense of it. *This isn't possible. This isn't real.*

But it was.

She stepped closer to the table, her heart hammering in her chest. Each letter she had written was no longer just a part of her past. It was now a piece of her present — something that had intertwined with the fabric of her reality, warping it in ways she couldn't undo. The letters had become more than just words; they had become a force, an uncontrollable power that was rewriting not just her history, but her future.

She glanced at the window, her eyes darting to the familiar view of the street outside. It had always been the same — the old house across the street, the overgrown garden, the lamppost that flickered at dusk. But today, the view was different. The street was empty, desolate, with no sign of life. The houses seemed distorted, as if someone had painted them in a hurry and hadn't bothered to let the paint dry.

Her mind was spinning. The walls seemed to stretch and shrink, the furniture warping in front of her eyes. She was standing still, yet everything around her was moving — shifting — as though it were being written and rewritten with every passing second.

She stumbled backward, her pulse quickening as she felt a wave of nausea rise in her chest. Was this what it meant to lose touch with reality? To be trapped in a world where nothing was certain, where everything was in constant flux?

She had created this. She had written herself into this world, and now she couldn't escape it. She had rewritten her past, her memories, her relationships — and now they were all colliding in a storm she couldn't control.

What have I done? The thought gnawed at her, sinking deeper into her mind. Every decision, every word had created ripples that had altered the course of everything. And the more she tried to fix it, the more she realized she was only making it worse.

She walked toward the mirror in the hallway, her reflection staring back at her — but it didn't look quite right. Her face was there, her eyes were there, but there was something off about it. The person in the mirror wasn't exactly the same person she saw in her mind. Her features were sharper, her expression colder, more distant.

For a moment, Alex didn't recognize herself. The person staring back at her wasn't the woman she had become. It was someone else — someone she had created.

Her hands trembled as she reached up, touching her face, almost as if trying to confirm that she was still real. *Is this me?* she thought. *Or is this a version of me that I've written?*

She turned away from the mirror, her mind whirling. The house was starting to feel like a maze, its walls closing in on her as she walked through the rooms, each one more unfamiliar than the last. She could hear the echoes of her own thoughts bouncing off the walls, but the words didn't make sense anymore. They were fragments, pieces of a story she couldn't finish.

She needed to understand. She needed to know if any of this was real, if any of it mattered. But the more she searched for answers, the more she realized that she was the one creating the story — and it was no longer a story she could control.

Alex collapsed onto the couch, burying her face in her hands, the weight of everything pressing down on her. *What if the past can never truly be rewritten?* The question hung in the air like a dark cloud. What if she couldn't fix what had been broken? What if the choices she had made had already sealed her fate?

The more she tried to rewrite the past, the more she realized she was losing herself in it. She had created a reality, but that reality had turned against her. It was too late to change it now.

Her mind felt like it was unraveling, slipping through her fingers like sand. She had been so determined to rewrite her life, to fix what had been wrong, but now she saw it clearly — the price of control. The more she tried to shape it, the more it slipped away. The past, the present, the future — they were all blending together, becoming one.

And in the end, it didn't matter how many words she wrote. She was trapped in a narrative of her own making, and there was no way out.

21

Chapter 20: The Final Confrontation

The house was silent, too silent. Alex sat in the same chair where she had first confronted the letters, her fingers clenched tightly around the arms of the seat. The air felt thick, heavy with the weight of the choices she had made. Everything had led her to this moment — the letters, the changes, the desperate attempts to rewrite the past. But now, the question was no longer about fixing the broken pieces. Now, it was about accepting the price she had paid.

What have I become?

The world around her seemed to pulse with an unnatural rhythm, each flicker of light, each subtle shift in the air, amplifying the dissonance in her mind. It was as if reality itself were on the verge of crumbling. She could feel it — the walls closing in on her, the foundation of everything she had built shaking, threatening to collapse.

The past, the present, the future — they had all blurred together. But now, there was only one thing left to do. She couldn't keep running from the truth. She couldn't keep trying to rewrite her life.

The figure appeared in the doorway, as it always did, but this time, it felt different. It wasn't just a shadow, an echo of her subconscious. It was *real*, standing there in the dim light of the room, its presence a force that consumed everything around her.

The Correspondent.

"You've written your story, Alex," the figure said, its voice calm, almost compassionate. "But now it's time to choose."

Alex's heart raced, and for a moment, she thought she might choke on her own breath. She stood up slowly, her legs unsteady as she faced the figure, the truth dawning on her like a heavy weight. *The choice.*

"You've already been given everything you wanted," the Correspondent continued. "The world has bent to your will. Your past, your memories — they're all malleable, shapeless, ready for you to mold. But now, Alex, you must decide."

Alex swallowed, her voice barely a whisper. "Decide? Decide what?"

"The choice," the Correspondent repeated, stepping closer, its shadow stretching across the room like a living thing. "You can continue living in the world you've created. A world where your past is perfect, where the mistakes are erased, where the people you've lost are still here. You can stay in this reality, this illusion of control, and leave everything behind."

Alex shook her head, her mind whirling. *A perfect world?* A world that she had created, but at what cost? Was it really worth it? Was it worth living in a reality that had no foundation, no truth?

"But there's another choice," the Correspondent continued, its voice growing colder. "You can let go of this world. You can face the reality you've long abandoned. The past that you've been running from. You can face yourself. The truth of who you really are, without the need to rewrite it. But it will come at a cost. Everything you've built, everything you've written, will be gone."

Alex's stomach twisted, a cold dread creeping over her. "But... if I let go... what's left? What's left if I go back to the truth?"

"The truth, Alex," the Correspondent said softly, "is what you've been avoiding. It's the one thing you've feared all along. The things you've lost, the things you can't change. The things you've tried to fix."

The figure stepped closer still, its presence overwhelming, like the weight of the entire world bearing down on her. "You have to choose: a life of illusion and control, or the painful truth of the past. You can't have both."

Alex stood there, frozen, as the words rang in her ears. *Illusion and control* — that's what she had created. She had built a world where the past was always within her grasp, where she could erase the mistakes, fix the broken parts of herself. But was it really worth it? Was it worth living in a world that didn't feel real, where every connection was fragile, and every moment was an artifice?

The weight of the decision pressed down on her. She closed her eyes, trying to breathe, trying to steady herself. The past was never going to be perfect. She had spent so long trying to make it so, but maybe... maybe the truth wasn't in rewriting it. Maybe it was in accepting it.

What would it be like to stop writing? To stop trying to control everything?

A wave of panic rose within her chest, but beneath it, something else began to stir. A flicker of clarity.

It was the truth she had been avoiding all along. The past couldn't be rewritten. The people she had lost couldn't be brought back. The mistakes, the regrets, the pain — they couldn't be erased.

But what if, just maybe, she could live with them? What if she could stop running from the truth and accept the life she had? *What if the story didn't need to be perfect to be worth living?*

She took a deep breath, her pulse racing, and looked at the Correspondent — at the version of herself that had been pulling the strings all along.

"I choose the truth," she said, her voice stronger than she expected. "I choose to face what's real, no matter how painful it is. I choose to let go of the illusion."

For a moment, the room was still. The figure stood silent, and then, finally, it nodded. "You've made your choice, Alex. The story you've written has ended."

The air in the room seemed to shift, the oppressive weight lifting ever so slightly. The Correspondent's form began to fade, the edges of the figure blurring like a dream slipping away.

Alex felt her legs give way beneath her, and she sank to the floor, her breath coming in sharp gasps. The truth was both freeing and terrifying. The world around her began to lose its sharpness, the edges of the house, the town, the memories — they all began to blur, as if the pages of her life were being erased, one by one.

But then, just as quickly, everything stilled.

The room, the house, the town outside — they were all the same, and yet... not. She could feel it. The reality she had chosen was hers, but it wasn't the one she had crafted with her words. It wasn't the world of perfect control. It was something real. Something raw. Something that she had finally accepted.

She was no longer writing. She was simply *living.*

And for the first time in a long time, it felt like the right choice.

22

Chapter 21: The End of the Story

The house was silent once again, but it was different this time. The walls, the familiar rooms, the chairs she had sat in and the table where she had written her past into existence — it all felt distant now, like a world she had outgrown. The air was no longer oppressive but still, the way the space felt after a storm had passed, when everything was suspended in a quiet calm.

Alex stood in the kitchen, her eyes fixed on the stack of letters on the table, the ones that had carried her deepest fears and desires, the ones that had rewritten her life over and over. Each letter had been a step toward something she thought she needed. Each word, each sentence had been a way to make sense of a past that never seemed to let go.

But now, they were just paper. They were just words. Words she had no longer needed.

The Correspondent, the figure who had once been her guide, her creation — it was gone. The presence that had lingered in the shadows, pulling the strings of her life, was fading, slipping away like a half-forgotten dream. Alex could feel it, the absence of that weight, the absence of the manipulation that had once seemed so certain, so omnipresent. The air was clearer now, less heavy with the weight of her own making.

She had made a choice. A choice that felt both final and freeing.

Without a second thought, Alex reached for the letters. One by one, she picked them up, holding them in her hands for a moment before crumpling them. The paper tore easily, a satisfying sound that echoed through the stillness. She had poured everything into these letters — her regrets, her pain, her longing. But now, they were just fragments of a world she no longer wanted to live in.

She stepped toward the stove, setting the small pile of crumpled paper into the metal tray beneath the flame. The fire flickered to life quickly, dancing hungrily across the edges of the paper. She watched as the letters curled and blackened, the words vanishing in the heat, the ink dissolving into ash.

For a long moment, Alex didn't move. She only stared at the flames, watching them consume everything she had written, everything she had believed in, until there was nothing left but smoke. The scent of burning paper filled the air, and as it did, Alex felt something inside her — a tightness in her chest, a knot that had been there for so long — begin to loosen.

It's over, she thought. *The story is finished.*

The last of the letters turned to ash, the flames dying down to embers. The fire was small now, just the remnants of something that had once been powerful, something she had once relied on to escape. But the escape was over. It had to be.

She stepped back from the stove, her heart pounding, her thoughts racing. The silence in the room was both terrifying and peaceful. It was the silence that came after the storm had passed, when everything was still, when the world was waiting for her to make the next move.

But she didn't need to write anymore. She didn't need to fix things, rewrite them, or change the past. What had been done, what had been lost, was part of her now. And for the first time in a long time, that felt like enough.

Alex closed her eyes, letting out a shaky breath. She had faced the truth, finally accepted the world she had tried to escape. The past couldn't be rewritten. It couldn't be erased. It could only be accepted. And for the first time, she wasn't afraid of that.

She opened her eyes and walked toward the door, the sound of her footsteps steady and sure against the floor. She opened it, stepping outside into the cool evening air. The town stretched before her, the houses standing tall against the horizon, the streets quiet and still. It was the same town, the same world she had tried so desperately to escape. But now, it felt different.

It felt real.

The shadows of the past were still there, but they no longer held the same power over her. She had accepted them, and with that acceptance, she had freed herself.

The Correspondent's voice, once so insistent, so commanding, was gone. There was no more whispering in the shadows, no more guidance from a hidden hand. The story was hers now. And she could write her own ending, her own future — without fear, without regret.

Alex stepped forward, the weight of the decision settling around her like the cool evening breeze. She didn't need the letters anymore. She didn't need to control everything, to rewrite everything. She just needed to live.

And for the first time, she knew that was enough.

23

Chapter 22: The Return

The air felt different when Alex stepped out of the cottage. It wasn't the oppressive weight she had grown used to, nor was it the cool, empty calm that followed the storm of her decision. No, this was something else entirely. The air felt... clearer, somehow. It was as if the fog that had clouded her mind had finally lifted, leaving behind a strange sense of peace, but also an undeniable sense of disorientation.

She had burned the letters. She had left behind the twisted world she had created, the version of her life she had so desperately tried to rewrite. And yet, as she stood there in the quiet of the morning, she couldn't shake the feeling that something was still wrong.

Her footsteps echoed on the gravel as she moved through the yard, the familiar landscape stretching out before her. The same old trees, the same crooked fence, the same path that led out of the cottage and into the heart of the town. It all looked the same. But it didn't *feel* the same.

The sun shone brighter than usual, casting a soft, golden glow across the town. She could hear the birds chirping, the distant murmur of wind in the trees. The world was waking up, but it was as if Alex had missed something. As if, in the act of leaving behind the world she had crafted, she had somehow stepped into something new — something just slightly off.

She took a deep breath and began walking, her feet carrying her down the familiar path toward the town. Each step felt heavier than the last, as if the earth beneath her was slowly pulling her back into a reality she had long forgotten. Or was it?

The town square came into view, and Alex's heart skipped a beat. Everything looked so... ordinary. The same old shops lined the street, the same tired faces shuffled past her, heads down as they moved through their daily routines. But as she stood there, at the edge of the square, she noticed something strange — no one seemed to notice her. Not in the way they once had.

She had spent years here, had built a life in this place. But now, it felt like she was a stranger. A passerby in a world that didn't truly belong to her anymore.

She walked past the bakery, the familiar smell of fresh bread wafting from the door. The same old bakery she had visited countless times, a place that had once felt like home. But now, even that felt different. The owner, an elderly man who had always smiled and nodded at her, didn't even look up when she passed. It was as though he didn't recognize her.

Alex paused, her breath catching in her throat. She turned back, her eyes scanning the bakery. It wasn't just the people who felt different. The town, her town, seemed... changed.

The sky had shifted too. The clouds were lighter, whiter, almost ethereal. The colors of the buildings, the houses — even the pavement underfoot — seemed brighter, somehow, more vivid, like someone had adjusted the saturation on a photograph. It was still the same world, yet it was as though someone had shifted its hue, just slightly, enough to make everything look unfamiliar.

She walked past the town square, towards the street that led to her childhood home. The house was just up ahead, its familiar silhouette standing against the backdrop of the town. But as she neared it, her steps slowed. Her chest tightened.

The house was different. It wasn't the house she remembered.

The front yard was tidier than it used to be, the porch newly painted, the hedges trimmed neatly, unlike the overgrown, wild garden she had known. The windows sparkled in a way they never had before, as if the house were newly built. The door — the door that had always been chipped and worn — was now smooth, freshly painted, almost pristine.

Her stomach twisted. She had grown up in this house. It had been a place of comfort and chaos, of memories both painful and precious. But now, it looked... wrong.

She reached the front step, hesitated, and knocked softly on the door. She couldn't explain why she was knocking — she had lived there for years, but now it felt like a strange place. She waited for the sound of footsteps inside, but when the door opened, it wasn't her mother, or her father, or anyone she expected.

It was a woman she didn't recognize — someone who looked at her with a faint, polite smile.

"Yes?" The woman's voice was warm but distant, as though she had no real connection to Alex.

"I... I used to live here," Alex said, her voice unsteady. "I grew up in this house."

The woman tilted her head, her smile faltering for just a moment. "I'm sorry," she said kindly, "but this house has been ours for several years now."

Alex's heart skipped a beat. "What do you mean? I—I used to live here. My parents..."

The woman's expression softened, though there was a hint of confusion in her eyes. "I'm not sure what you mean. We've lived here for quite a while now."

Alex stood there for a moment, dumbfounded. She turned away from the door, feeling the weight of the words sinking in. *Several years?* The house — her home — had been taken over by someone else. Her parents, the family she had known, weren't here. They weren't in the house anymore.

Her mind reeled. She had lived here. She had built memories here. But now, it seemed as though those memories were being erased, fading into something she could no longer touch.

She walked away from the house, her footsteps heavy as she moved back down the street. The town, the people, her home — everything felt like it was slipping through her fingers, like sand falling from her hands. She had rewritten her past, tried to fix what had been broken, but now it felt as though she had lost it all.

The town was still there. The buildings, the trees, the streets — they were all still in place. But it wasn't *her* town anymore. It was a parallel reality, a world that had changed in ways she couldn't fully comprehend.

She had been so focused on rewriting her past, on erasing the pain, the mistakes, and the regrets. But now, she was left with a world that no longer felt like hers. A world where the past, no matter how much she tried to reshape it, had been lost forever.

And as she stood there in the middle of the street, watching the world she had once known, Alex realized the truth: *You can't rewrite the past. You can't undo what's been done. The past, no matter how much you try to control it, is gone.*

And perhaps that was the greatest truth of all — that in trying to fix everything, she had lost everything.

The town stretched before her, unchanged and yet completely different. And Alex had no idea where she belonged anymore.

24

Chapter 23: The Echo of the Correspondent

The silence of the morning stretched out before Alex like a fragile veil, one that could tear at any moment. After all she had been through — the letters, the rewrites, the confrontations with the Correspondent — she thought she had finally stepped into a reality where she could breathe again. A reality where the past, no matter how painful, would remain just that — the past.

But as she moved through her new life, the weight of uncertainty never truly left her. The town still felt foreign, even after days of wandering through its familiar streets, trying to find something to anchor her. The changes were small, almost imperceptible, but they were enough to make her feel like a stranger in her own world.

She had thought she could outrun the echoes of her decisions, that she could find peace in the blank slate she had desperately sought. But peace, it seemed, was a fleeting illusion. It was too easy to think that she had escaped the pull of the Correspondent, that the games were over.

But the game was never over.

It was in the small, mundane moments that it crept back in. The ordinary things she had taken for granted — opening a drawer, sorting through the papers in her desk — all felt different. Every motion felt deliberate, as though she were playing a role in some larger narrative, even if she didn't want to be.

It happened on a morning that felt too ordinary to be significant, just after she had returned to the small apartment she had rented in the town. The sun streamed through the window, casting long, warm beams of light across the table. Alex had been sorting through a box of her belongings, trying to settle in, when she found it.

A single letter, tucked away among her old things. It was a simple envelope, aged and slightly crinkled, the paper yellowed with time. At first, Alex thought it was just another piece of forgotten correspondence from her old life, but as she picked it up, the air around her seemed to shift. She recognized the handwriting immediately.

The same precise script, the same delicate strokes, the same ink that had filled the pages of every letter she had ever written to herself, to others, to the past.

The handwriting of the Correspondent.

Her heart skipped in her chest as she ripped open the envelope, her fingers trembling. Her eyes scanned the page quickly, the words searing into her mind.

> *Dear Alex,*
>
> *You thought you could outrun me. You thought you could erase the story and start fresh. But the truth is, the game is never over. You are still a player, whether you choose to acknowledge it or not. Every choice you make, every action you take, is a part of the game.*
>
> *You can try to change the past, rewrite it, burn it all away — but the truth is, you are bound to this story. You created it. You gave it life. And no matter how far you run, no matter how much you try to escape, the narrative will find you.*
>
> *So tell me, Alex, what will you do now? Will you continue writing,*

> *continue rewriting? Or will you let the game play out and accept the consequences? The choice is still yours. But remember — there is no escaping the game. There is no end.*

The words blurred in her vision as Alex felt her stomach twist. She had hoped, prayed, that by choosing the truth, by burning the letters, she had severed the connection. That she had finally freed herself from the hold of the Correspondent. But here, in this quiet room, in the life she had tried to rebuild, the echo of the game was still there.

She stood frozen, the letter slipping from her hand as the weight of the message sank in. The Correspondent's presence, once a shadow in the background of her life, was now unmistakable. She had thought it was over. She had thought she was free.

But the truth was, she hadn't really left the game. The rules hadn't changed. They never did.

Alex stared at the letter on the floor, her thoughts racing, the walls of the room pressing in on her once more. She had believed that by letting go of the past, by stopping the cycle of rewriting, she could finally live in the present. But now, she realized that she had been mistaken. She had only been given the illusion of freedom.

The game was still being played. And she had never been in control.

The letter wasn't just a reminder. It was a declaration. The Correspondent had never really left. It wasn't a voice that could be silenced, not a force that could be outwritten. The story had no end — only an endless cycle of decisions and consequences.

And Alex, for all her attempts to break free, was still a part of it.

She could feel it, a creeping sense of dread rising in her chest as the weight of the truth settled in. She wasn't free. She was still being watched, still being led by an unseen hand.

The question lingered, hanging in the air like a fog: *What will you do now?*

But Alex already knew the answer. There was no end to this. No real escape. The only question left was whether she would continue to write, to play along, or whether she would accept that the game had no final move, no final victory — only the endless turn of the page.

She had always been a player. And the game had only just begun.

25

Chapter 24: The Final Letter

The letter sat on the table in front of Alex, the pen poised over it, its weight almost too heavy to bear. She had thought it was over. She had thought that when she made the choice to face the truth, when she burned the letters, when she stopped trying to rewrite her past, that would be the end of it.

But as the days passed and the echo of the Correspondent's voice lingered in her mind, it became clear — the game was never truly over. It was still playing out. She could feel it, creeping in with every thought, every step she took.

But this time, Alex wouldn't play. Not anymore.

The room around her felt heavy, suffocating. She had done everything she could to let go of the world she had crafted — the stories, the rewriting, the desperate attempts to fix things that couldn't be fixed. She had tried so hard to control it all, and every time she did, it slipped further from her grasp.

But not anymore.

Her grip on the pen tightened, her mind clear for the first time in days. The game, the Correspondent, the world she had rewritten over and over again — it was all a prison. And now, Alex was ready to break free.

She didn't need a long, drawn-out declaration. She didn't need to explain herself anymore. She had learned that the more words she used, the more she fed the cycle, the more she fed the game. So, this letter would be different.

This letter would be brief. This letter would say everything.

I choose silence.

She wrote the words quickly, the ink flowing onto the paper, sharp and final. Her hand didn't tremble. Her mind didn't race. There was no hesitation. It was simple, direct.

She chose silence. She chose to stop playing.

Alex set the pen down and stared at the letter for a long moment. The room seemed still, as if waiting for something. She didn't know what would happen next, but she was ready. The Correspondent had controlled her life for far too long, had whispered in the background of every decision she made, every letter she wrote. But she was done.

She folded the letter carefully, smoothing the creases before standing and walking toward the door. For the first time, she didn't feel the weight of the world pressing down on her. She felt light, unburdened, as though she had let go of something that had been holding her down for a long time.

With the letter in hand, she stepped outside, into the quiet world beyond. The town seemed different somehow, but it wasn't the same strange world it had once been. It felt real, like the past and present had finally settled into something stable.

She didn't need the Correspondent anymore. She didn't need to be controlled, to be a player in someone else's game. She had made her choice. The silence was her answer. It was her final statement.

And as Alex walked down the street, the letter clutched in her hand, she knew that the story was over — her story, her life, the one she had been writing all this time. She had chosen silence, and with it, freedom.

26

Chapter 25: The Silence

The world was still.

The silence stretched on, deeper than it had ever been before. Alex stood in the middle of the street, the letter from the Correspondent still in her hand, now crumpled slightly from the tight grip she had held it with. The town — the same town she had lived in for so long, the same streets she had walked a hundred times — now felt like a different place. The noise, the bustle, the life that had always filled it was absent, leaving only a quiet, pervasive emptiness.

And for the first time, Alex didn't mind the silence. In fact, it was comforting. It felt like a balm after the storm of confusion, of rewriting, of trying to control everything that was beyond her reach. It was the silence she had been searching for — the one that existed outside of the game, outside of the manipulation.

The town was still. The air hung heavy, unmoving, as if waiting for something that would never come.

Alex's heart pounded in her chest as she looked at the people around her. They moved through the streets as they always had — some with their heads down, others chatting with friends, others simply walking by, lost in their own world. But there was something different about them, something that Alex couldn't quite put her finger on. It was as though they were distant, as though they were a part of something she could no longer touch, no longer influence.

A cold shiver ran through her.

She looked down at the crumpled letter in her hand. The words she had written to the Correspondent — her declaration of silence — had been the end of something. But what had it ended?

The world still felt like it was waiting for something, and Alex suddenly realized that it wasn't the world that was waiting. It was *her*. She was the one who had been waiting. Waiting for permission. Waiting for answers. Waiting for someone else to take control of her story.

But no one else had been in control.

The realization hit her all at once, the last piece of the puzzle falling into place with a sharp clarity.

The Correspondent had never existed.

The presence, the figure that had loomed over her every decision, the voice that had whispered in her mind, pushing her to write, to reshape, to control — it had all been her. It had always been her.

Alex had been the one writing her story, rewriting her reality with every word she put to paper. The Correspondent wasn't a figure in the shadows, a manipulator pulling the strings. It was the part of herself she had refused to acknowledge, the part of herself that had been controlling her life through the act of writing.

She had always been the one in charge.

The words she had written — the letters, the confessions, the stories — they had created this world. Every change, every shift, every distortion had been her doing. And now, as she stood there, the weight of it all settling in, Alex understood: The Correspondent was just a manifestation of her own need to control, her own need to rewrite the past.

She had created the illusion of another force, another presence, to blame for everything. But the truth was, it had always been her.

The power, the control, the manipulation of reality — it had always been in her hands.

Alex's breath caught in her throat as the weight of that truth settled over her. The silence around her was no longer oppressive. It was freeing. She had been so focused on writing, on trying to fix what had been broken, that she hadn't realized the power she had all along. She had always been the writer. She had always been the one who could choose the story.

And now, as she stood on the quiet street, Alex realized something else: *The story is over when the writer stops writing.*

The words had been her escape, her creation, her prison. But now, in this silence, in this stillness, she was no longer bound by them. She had stopped writing. She had chosen silence. And with that choice, she was finally free.

The town around her felt real again — not perfect, not rewritten, but real. It was a world that had never needed fixing, never needed rewriting. It was just life. *Her* life.

The weight of the letters, the stories, the need for control was gone. The Correspondent had never existed. It had been a part of herself she had finally let go of. And now, for the first time, Alex was free to live — not in a world she had written, but in a world that simply *was.*

As she took a deep breath, the air felt fresh, crisp. The silence was no longer just the absence of sound. It was the absence of need, the absence of the constant urge to rewrite what couldn't be rewritten.

The story was over.

And Alex, for the first time in a long time, felt like she had finally come home.

www.ingramcontent.com/pod-product-compliance
Lightning Source LLC
Chambersburg PA
CBHW031706170426
43345CB00012B/418

* 9 7 9 8 2 1 5 7 3 0 6 3 8 *